P9-ASH-531

The Plug of Lil Mexico

Chris Green

Lock Down Publications and Ca$h Presents

The Plug of Lil Mexico

A Novel by *Chris Green*

Chris Green

Lock Down Publications
P.O. Box 944
Stockbridge, Ga 30281

Visit our website @
www.lockdownpublications.com

Copyright 2021 by Chris Green
The Plug of Lil Mexico

All rights reserved. No part of this book may be reproduced in any form or by electronic or mechanical means, including information storage and retrieval systems without permission in writing from the publisher, except by a reviewer who may quote brief passages in review.
First Edition January 2022
Printed in the United States of America

This is a work of fiction. Names, characters, places, and incidents either are products of the author's imagination or are used fictitiously. Any similarity to actual events or locales or persons, living or dead, is entirely coincidental.

Lock Down Publications
Like our page on Facebook: Lock Down Publications @
www.facebook.com/lockdownpublications.ldp

Book interior design by: **Shawn Walker**
Edited by: **Kiera Northington**

4

Stay Connected with Us!

Text **LOCKDOWN** to 22828 to stay up-to-date with new releases, sneak peaks, contests and more…

Thank you!

Submission Guideline

Submit the first three chapters of your completed manuscript to ldpsubmissions@gmail.com, subject line: Your book's title. The manuscript must be in a .doc file and sent as an attachment. Document should be in Times New Roman, double spaced and in size 12 font. Also, provide your synopsis and full contact information. If sending multiple submissions, they must each be in a separate email.

Have a story but no way to send it electronically? You can still submit to LDP/Ca$h Presents. Send in the first three chapters, written or typed, of your completed manuscript to:

LDP: Submissions Dept
Po Box 944
Stockbridge, Ga 30281

DO NOT send original manuscript. Must be a duplicate.

Provide your synopsis and a cover letter containing your full contact information.

Thanks for considering LDP and Ca$h Presents.

A word from Smokey Carter

First of all, I would like to thank my mama and all of my children and God. Uncle Slip Rock, of course White Boy Keith. My boy Lil Rico. My daughter Rykira and Armonie. I would like to thank everyone that supported me in this mix of the book coming about. I would like to thank my dad T. This will be a journey for the next book. I would like to thank my baby mamas. The ones that still stood down and got my kids to go get in the right direction. Two graduated and one on the way.

Chris Green

Prologue

1017 Peeple Street, SW Atlanta

West End aka NiggaVille

It had been months since we've had peace in the house. and today was it. Today was damn sho it. The heater had been broken since yesterday, and I had to deal with the fact of my son wailing his ass off, due to the conditions of my family's lack of home maintenance.

I rocked lil Smoke gently in my arms as I waited patiently at the window for my lying ass best friend to come get me and release the torturing tension on my mental but dealing with the bullshit was something I'd adapted to after some time. At fifteen, I had been through more shit than the average grown ass woman had yet to experience. True enough, I wasn't able to care for myself completely how I wanted to. It left the stanky ass wheel in my people's hands. That basically put it up to me hold on and get a mighty dollar how I could.

It was all for Smoke, especially when you were living under another being's roof, and eating up a lil groceries. My newborn son was only five months, and I've stomped through the fire and caught all the hell the devil had to auction off from my father's wrath since he'd been born."

The sound of my step mama's bedroom door cracked, and I turned to face her. From the look, she was still stuck on the small dispute from earlier. She came out the doorway, hissing and smacking like usual. Her big ole Gucci nightgown hung to the floor like a queen's robe, as she was awakening from the throne. Her hair was French curled in a roll, and the make-up she was working looked a tad bit wet as if it had just been applied. It was even funnier because my father has money, spoils her dearly, but shoves the shoulder when I needed help with his grandson. The guy that spat me out the old sack.

"Lil girl, you must can't read?"

A hand was on her hip with a turned-up nose like JJ from *Good Times*. Of course, I didn't want to argue with the queen of authority, so I tried to be polite.

"What do you mean? Of course, I can read." I flashed a nasty mug as if my eyebrows were able to punch this annoying ass lady out her comfort zone.

"That damn *AJC* newspaper got all them job sightings in there. Cashiers, table girls. The wash. That thing getting cold and stiff from laying there, try picking it up!"

She was yelling so loud, I couldn't do anything but sit in silence, like she was insane. Hell, she was insane. Practically the whole family was. I just didn't want to argue, and Smokey was just on his way to sleep. I was just about to comment, and my father's footsteps came walking into the home, with his tie hung loose and mode on slump.

"Oh, you must didn't hear what I asked you to do, Toria? Now that your father is home, I'll allow him to see this horrible side of you." Her crooked, Salem cigarette-stained fronts was grinning all twisted.

"Vee, how many times do we have to go through this? Methea is like your biological mother. You obey her when told to do so." He dropped his suitcase with a daring tone, and I could sense his day at work had been shitty.

"I've done nothing wrong. She's edging me on, and she knows it."

"No buts, young lady. We aren't doing the back and forth, young child. That's a warning." He stuck out his stubby index finger, pointing at me for assurance to know he wasn't talking to anybody else.

You know I had a fly ass mouth like the wings on a birds back, and before I could catch my temper from flying off the handle, I bit the bait.

"I have a whole child, I'm surely not about to be sitting here arguing with no grown folks." I stormed off with Smokey, headed for the room.

I didn't see my father's expression when he said it, but his look was damn sure clear in my mind.

"Victoria Carter, this is the last time I will allow you to disrespect the rules of my home. You're only fifteen, and you're as loose as a cannon with your attitude. You don't feel like listening to us is the correct way. Well, guess what? Take the second option I whipped up in the box. You got fifteen minutes to pack ya shit and disappear out my home. You, and Smokey. You feel grown. Hit me up when you feel a year of some bills!"

I faced him with tears welling in my eyes because Smokey had just begun to settle in my arms, when the disparaging remark shot daggers through my chest. I nearly dropped my son on the tile floor. Things were beyond serious, because he moved towards the front door with a purpose. Opening it with a straight face. He stood silently, as if the words, "Get out," wasn't necessary.

I kept it pushing upstairs, packed a few things for me and the baby, and found myself standing in front of the West End train station ten minutes later. If it wasn't just good luck, it started to pour down raining, barely leaving shelter for me and my child to stand under. I cried for the first four hours, pondering on what to do as I walked the entire southwest. After pushing up Avon, Lockwood, and Elizabeth Street for the hundredth time, I found myself directly back in front of the train station with the same distraught gaze.

The light giggles from Smokey forced me to look down at him, chilling in the stroller. He was batting his eyes at me like it was just for sure things was gonna be alright. My mind was running to a thousand places, while I pondered on a location to lay my head until I got the right change in my pockets. I wasn't too far from giving in when I finally stood to leave, and that's when I spotted the 1976 big body Cadillac pulling in front of me. I knew niggas was quick to rape some shit, around the SWATS, and Boo Boo the Fool damn sure wasn't my name.

The passenger window rolling down stopped me in my tracks, especially after the comment that came behind it.

"Mama V, I thought we was on one accord about you walking around this hood. You know I can't protect you if I can't keep sight of you."

Huffing with a light smile, my heartbeat sped up. His eyes were locked in on me, like a child struggling with homework, and I knew he damn sure wasn't into the school life.

"What do you want T?" I asked, not trying to entertain his charming game at that moment.

He flashed a confident thirty-two, before putting the car in park to jump out, standing six-two with a light husky build. He rocked a low cut. He was draped in a pair of crispy blue jeans, a gray Coogi sweater, and I know the Audemar watch dangling from his wrist had to be at least a couple thousand. His aura wasn't arrogant, but strong enough to see money was far from a problem.

"Any reasons why you out here with lil man in this weather?" He folded his arms all cool-like.

I didn't wanna show the slump in my mood, so I threw it off with a smirk. "Why you so worried? Don't you got like thirteen lil hunnies you need to pick up in that pimp mobile of yours.

"Hunnies? I don't even think the bunnies got enough time for me. My tongue be stuck up my money's ass too much, V. Plus, I already told you, I'm from Miami. We love our ladies like newborn babies."

I couldn't help but to share a laugh with him. It was always some smooth shit coming behind his words. I just wished trusting it one hundred percent truly stood within my bounds. My biological child's father proclaimed to be the ultimate with loyalty and raising Smoke. I didn't find out that was a lie, until he ditched us after Smokey was born. That was a day I never wanted to relive. Hell, I was barely living my own life.

"I'm only fifteen with a whole baby. Why you chasing me, T? You nineteen, chasing me with all that money, and another baby mama. How can I possibly fit into the equation of that?"

My question puzzled him, and he lowered his eyes at all my small bags and rolling suitcase. I could usually read what was on a dude's mind when it came to running the game. With him, it was hard to even know whether guessing existed. He leaned down, brushing his fingers on Smokey's sleeping head. I was even more shocked when he picked him up and held out his other hand to me.

"T, what are you doing? Put my baby down, boy. I got enough going on already." I slick begged just so he wouldn't agitate me like other dudes tried often.

"I know you got enough going on, which is why I'm about to make sure you about to do a little bit of nothing from now on. I told you I would take care of you if you gave me the chance. You're smart for your age, and that's the only key allowing us to hold a bond. You gotta trust me though." He extended his hand once more for me to rise off the bench.

I'm not gonna lie as if I didn't hesitate. The known pretty boy swag was easily conniving, but my son resting peacefully in this same fool's arms was too good for my sight to see. Smokey didn't just let no anybody hold him, and his assuring face made me wonder if he really wanted to help to me.

"How do you know you can make me happy? What if you can't help me?" I glanced out into the evening traffic of the West End four-way.

"Look at you. You're gorgeous. If I can't, I'm sure any lucky, smart cat would be honored just to try, love." He chuckled like I was overthinking my future.

Standing up to match his energy. I took a deep breath. "Just please never leave me stranded like a fool and lie. If that's not in your plan, you'll keep me 'til death. If it is, you gone wish like hell it was the first thing on yo list." I grabbed my things, heading for the car.

I made one thing I didn't know on my disastrous day of turmoil. A hard road of a new life but met a man that was gonna provide at any cost.

Just as our car exited the train station's parking lot, a round of gunshots exploded through the rear window. I instantly knew as I cradled Smoke in my arms, I was now convicted to a man with strong underworld ties. The dealer himself, Miami T.

Chapter 1

Miami, Florida, six years later

Smoke

As I stared out the window of my bedroom, I waited to see my dad's car pull through the driveway. It was never like him to be late coming home, on family-time night. We usually kicked it and watched a few movies, after he ordered takeout on his off days, like every weekend for the past two years. Along with me, my brother OJ, and twin sisters Bee and VeeBaby. My oldest brothers Anthony and Christopher stayed with us also. Children from another secret woman T was with before he moved me and my mama down by the water.

I knew she cursed him a lot for doing wrong but coming through as a father was something he was more than good at. I truly just didn't want my day to end without catching him before he jumped back to the streets. Little did I know that was gonna be my last day in Miami as a child.

Making my way out the room, I bumped dead into Linda, Dad's other girlfriend. She stayed with us also. We never spoke much, and she rarely was there, but I still showed respect for my father.

"Any dirty laundry in dere?" She looked at me a with a raised eyebrow like I was up to something.

"No, ma'am. My mama washed them all yesterday." I moved past her quickly, heading down the short flight of steps. My dad stayed in a four-bedroom townhome down the street from the beach. I didn't know anyone in my neighborhood too much, besides the close houses that always seemed to be watching.

As I got to the bottom level of my father's home, I spotted my mother in the guest area, sipping on a small flute glass, bopping back and forth like she just got a settlement. I always loved to see her happy because it surely hurt me to see somebody do her wrong.

"Hey, Mama. What you so happy fo?" I questioned, not really caring too much about the answer.

Pinching my cheek firmly, she kissed my forehead. "I just want to protect you all, baby boy. Mama accepting a lot to make sure y'all can cheese back at me. I'm just praying it can get a little better, to where we ain't gotta worry about worry bothering us anymore. Take out the trash for me, baby, will you?" Her tone trailed off sadly, before heading upstairs.

I knew something was bothering my mama, and I kinda felt like I knew what it was. She hated when he didn't come home because she always said it was a sign of choosing the streets over your family. He looked at it as lounge around like a deadbeat or feed the family. My mom, and even stepmother, never spoke on it. No matter how much money we had saved Dad just wouldn't stay out the streets. It made me kinda wonder, *what was he doing*? I thought quietly to myself as tied the filthy glad bag in a knot.

You could smell old Chinese food leaking from the plastic, but my light arms were able to tote it down to the curbbie, before catching my breath. My eyes happened to spot my dad's Range Rover parked two houses down in front of the idiots of the street, the Haitians. Two more cars were directly behind, parked.

Moving a little closer, I trailed out our huge front yard and walked a few feet down, to make sure I wasn't seeing things. The white Jesus hands in the windshield told me I was right after I got to a closer distance. It was crazy, because Daddy always told me to stay far away from the dread heads. I knew if his car was there, he had to be inside the large, one-level home.

Skipping up through the driveway across the light patch of grass, a few dogs barked, and the moon was starting to reach the peak. I got to the entrance, and for some reason, I started to instantly catch light chills. Shaking it off, I just knocked hard on the front door five times and waited. It felt like hours went by and I hadn't heard a peep.

Walking deeper on the porch, a loud scream erupted from inside the home. My heart said to get up out of there, but my pride wasn't about to let nothing happen to my dad. Spotting the corner window, I took baby steps towards it, and peeked in. The sight of T holding a gun to a bloody Haitian's forehead forced me to double take. Three more men with masks stood behind him with guns also.

I couldn't make out what they were saying, but I'd never seen my dad act the way he performed. He snarled like a beast in the man's face and pointed the gun. The first shot was louder than thunder, and seven more shots rang out right behind it. The sight of his blood spilling turned my stomach, and his body crashed face first into the floor on impact.

Turning around, I struck out of the yard like the speed of a greyhound. I didn't want to look back, and I definitely didn't want to T to know what I'd seen. I just knew someone was bound to snatch me up at any second as I broke back for my home.

Running through the back door. I shot past my sisters and brothers in the kitchen, headed straight for my room. I slammed the door behind me and placed my back against the door to make sure no one came in at the second. My heart was beating three different ways, and I knew my dad did some things that would get you caged in the cell forever. He always told me, "Never to talk to anybody but your lawyer, and God." To hear, not even telling him my secrets, regardless of problems. At six going on seven, his many problems I could truly have.

The sound of sirens, and a loud helicopter had my eyes on the window like a postage note. The trail of eight Miami police officers was flushing down our street like bats, plus a black double-lighted chopper was in the air, rotating in the area for search of any nearby bad guys. I kept my attention on them, until they pulled directly in front of the Haitian man's crib. My father's car was still parked there, and eight different officers was now running through the yard with guns out.

All it took was thirty seconds tops to bring a ram, and the front door was down, with tear gas tossed in immediately. All officers lined up behind one another, pushing in with masks and guns raised. I watched the few police that stood back watching.

The sound of three more shots erupted, echoing through the sky, and the police started to scramble inside at a frenzy.

Rushing downstairs to see if my mama was aware, I found her posted on the porch, staring in confusion.

"What the hell is going on over here? Smokey, I need you to step back inside, baby." She brushed me off, with a swatting hand.

Doing as I was told, I headed for the living room, and posted with the rest of my brothers and sisters. We watched my mama and Linda have a few private discussions, even on the phone as we waited to see what had occurred.

After an hour of TV, the house grew quiet, and the sound of our back door cracking open forced my mama to jump up. A few seconds later, T came around the corner with a stunned face. Looking from side to side, he grabbed my mama, hugging her waist. "I'm sorry, Vee." He was breathing hard, and the blood specks on his shoes said it all.

"T, what the hell is going on? Cops were just all over the street. Mitch and Corey got arrested in that house, and one of them pulled a gun. The news said they were gunned down. Where you there?" she questioned him, clenching her jaws tighter than a boxer.

He rubbed a hand through his head before kissing her hand softly.

"Listen, I don't have time to argue, V. I want you to take the car. There's a hundred and fifty grand in the trunk. Get a hotel for a few days, and head back up to Atlanta until you hear from me. Take the kids and Linda. I need you out of here by tonight. Do you understand?" He stared into my mama's eyes sincerely.

She didn't fuss or frown at his request, instead she nodded, and turned to face me. "Smokey, I need you to wake your sisters and brothers. Tell them to be packed in five minutes. We're leaving," she added, shaking her head.

Doing what I was told, I gathered a few of my things, and made it back for the living room. T appeared downstairs in changed clothes, and a Louis Vuitton sack tossed across his back. Approaching me, he kneeled down, and rubbed my head hard. "How you feeling, baby boy?"

"Okay, I guess. Why we leaving?" I looked up into his eyes to see if he would spill the truth.

"Smokey, Miami is just starting to get a little too hot for us to stay any longer. We've had fun but going back to Atlanta will put us at a better position. I know you wanna see your grandma, and cousins when we touch down up there now. Keep ya chin up and protect your mama. You the man of the house, right?" He asked me that question like I was grown, and ready to take on the world. Still in all, I knew what he meant.

"Yeah, I am, Dad."

Good. That means you a solid man. Remember to stand, whether I'm here or not, because these lives in here are based off how we protect. I'm gonna be gone for a few days, but when I get back, I got something for you." He held out his hand for a shake.

"I gotcha, Dad." I agreed with a nod, even though I wasn't one hundred percent sure what size shoes I was about to step in. All I know is if it was said by my father, T, then every syllable was golden.

Kissing me with a hug, he did the same to all my brothers and sisters. My mother and Linda were last. He pulled them both in for passionate cuddles, and a few soft pecks apiece.

"I love you both dearly, despite all differences. We still living, so that's proof we doing something right. We stick together because you can do a lot with a team, alone just leaves you guessing for answers you eventually got to ask someone else. Do it for me, our kids, and growing family to come. It's time to get outta here," he stated, before revealing the gun behind his back. A different piece from the trigger he just pulled.

He rubbed my mama's stomach in a circle. She was two months pregnant, meaning another sibling was on the way for the fourth, or fifth time. It's a lot of us in this bunch, if you know what I mean.

"We can talk when you arrive in Atlanta." My mama grabbed the bags and led us all out to the driveway. Loading up inside the van, VeeBaby instantly started to complain before Mama could pull off.

"Mommy. How long is this gonna be?"

"Hey, Vee B, no questions right now, please. I need all you to listen up, because I don't need no extra backtalk on what I say." She was turned around in her front seat, eyes wide as an owl as she spoke. "It's time to leave Miami for good. We're going back to Atlanta. Whatever you little ones heard down here, or saw, stays down here. All we got is family, but understanding is everything."

She spat her peace before cranking up and pulling out the driveway. I spotted T watching us from the window, and we locked eyes for a brief moment. That was the moment I knew I would be a true hard head for the paper. I'll fast forward to the gutta.

Chris Green

Chapter 2

West End Atlanta, GA

Smoke

It had been hell on the scale since we moved back to Atlanta. Of course, my mama wanted to lay low, and my dad warned her about slowly spending the savings, just in case people got to watching her a little too hard. My grandma on People Street, ended up taking us back in as usual, and now I was getting older, the streets was my new bicycle.

T had been back and forth to see us but got on the radar with the feds. Months started to go by before we would get an answer from him, and then he would pop out of nowhere like it was Christmas. That had slowed down for the last year, and I knew it was because he was serving a few months in the county, under an alias for a pistol charge. She hated he was away for a small moment, but happier he wasn't taking a trip to Miami for a life sentence.

"Aye, Smokey, Mama calling you downstairs." OJ walked past me standing in the bathroom mirror.

"I'm coming." I snapped out the small daze I was in and finished washing my face.

One thing I could say about the elders in my family, they were providers, and that's the same energy that made me into the young dollar chaser I was at that moment. Since the fourth grade at Ragsdale Elementary, I had a fetish for keeping something in my pocket. T showed me well with that. I did everything possible around my way, now that I was able to cross the street alone. True enough, it was still dangerous like Miami, but the guys from the block, and the Muslim community nearly protected the entire neighborhood.

I made my way to the bottom floor and noticed the front door was open. Sunlight blazed through the entrance, forcing me to raise my hand. I stepped outside, and laid eyes on my mama, looking all fabulous on that bright Sunday.

My mama was always laced with a bright smile. Caramel skin, with fluffy long hair that was usually curled, she was wearing a yellow sundress, with a pair of one-inch, open-toed Dior slides.

"Wassup, Mama, where you going out to all jazzed up?" I kissed her cheek, tryna make sure no outsider didn't think about making no intentions on sliding in our family lane.

"Stop being so nosey." She popped the back of my head lightly. "I'm going out to handle some business. Watch after your brothers and sisters, and if any cops come here, or try to stop you—"

"I don't know where my dad is." I finished her sentence before she could go on. Being on point was like protocol in our walls. It was part of my guide when I was out in the streets moving around.

After nodding to me with approval, my mama jumped inside of her short-body green Lexus, pulling off.

I waited until her car bent the corner, and immediately took off on my own mission. Starting off walking through the hood, I busted a few back streets, speaking to a few individuals my people knew. I made sure to keep it pushing without staying in one spot too long. That was and easy way to be a victim to the cops, whether you were grown, or twelve years old, like I was at that time. I only had one mission on my mental when I played out in the hood for hours, to come back home with more than I had the day before.

The first place I made my stop was the West End Mall. It was always easy to catch somebody that needed quick help for a buck, with all the traffic that flowed around morning time. Of course, there was a young hustler posted on each corner, the bootlegging CD man was running around making a few sales, and the city was shining brighter than a Rolex watch on a junkie's wrist.

After stopping at the local grocery store, I asked a few civilians to carry their bags to the car in exchange for a lil payment. My first three targets shut me down fast, without even looking back. After a few cool twenty minutes, I found my lucky winners. A couple was coming out with their shopping cart, and both of their faces looked past exhausted.

"Excuse me." I raised my hand, putting on my best smile.

"Wassup, young man? You mind telling me why you jumping all in front of me, and my wife?" He stopped to hear me out.

I could see his woman was looking good, and his inquisitive expression made me get straight to the point. "I mean no harm, sir, but I am trying to see if I could maybe load your basket in the car for a small fee?"

"Hmm, how small?" This nigga folded his arms like he could cut me a professional NFL check or something. I was about to spit out five hundred, but decided to be more serious, just in case he thought of turning me down.

"Just five dollars."

"Damn, lil man. A whole five. That's kinda steep for a real OG like me."

"That's kinda cheap for a youngin like me," I replied with a smirk.

"Yes, you can, sweetie. I would love your help, and I'm gonna give you twenty." His wife smiled, placing the money into my palm.

I watched this nigga toot his nose all up, like he was ready to backhand her or something. Giving her a wink, I grabbed the buggy from her husband and started to push towards the car. After loading the trunk and handling my end of the bargain, I made my way back to the spot where I was just standing and picked the wallet up that fell out of his pocket. He was so busy checking me on his radar scale, he never seen his lifeline drop from his pants.

Picking it up, I spread it open, viewing the crispy bills inside. My hands instantly started to sweat, and I wasted no time stuffing it down into my pocket without counting. I didn't need Mr. Save 'Em pulling back up looking for me, but just in case if he pondered on the idea, I was gonna be long gone.

It was the year 1984, so the hood and city was only based off one thing. Reputation, and getting money. I was actually a young head, that can say I've been around the city of Atlanta, more than a few gangsta's that supposedly had made a name for themselves. Been through some of the toughest projects, from Bowen Homes to English Manor, and even Etheridge, and I still had yet to slow down with seeing the true way our hood, raised the next generations up. We were all destined for one thing. To have a hustle, or either struggle.

Strolling down Avon Street, I kept my eyes on the road to ensure my mama didn't up and bypass me. She knew if I was out this early in the a.m., then I was about to stick my nose into something that probably didn't smell too good. That was just a trait my mama knew I would have as I got older.

Chapter 3

The Junkyard

Oakland City, SW Atlanta

It had been at least six hours with me moving around the neighborhood for my come-up, and I had yet to make it back towards the crib. The sun was starting to drop and that just meant the city lights were about to start flashing.

Walking into the parking lot of my Uncle Slip Rock's establishment, I smiled just looking at all the movement. Beautiful women moved about freely, some barely having on enough clothes to cover their bodies. A few young thugs posted up with their guns in hand, and every type of luxury car you could muster up in your mind was parked inside the doublewide driveway. Mercedes, Porches, and a few Cadillac trucks. It was like a Beverly Hills spot, minus the rich, arrogant neighbors that loved to call the cops. Everyone in the town migrated to the junkyard if you were somebody, and if you weren't, then you obviously weren't in the right loop.

"Lil T, boy, what the hell you doing down here at the bottom side? Vee know you creeping this far away from the pad?" I heard a deep voice behind me.

I turned my neck, noticing one of my uncle's right-hand men, Kaddy Ko. Tall, brown-skinned nigga that moved slower than a turtle, but quick and dangerous about his bread. He was usually quiet, but always sipped on a bottle, and smoked cigarettes like it was no tomorrow.

"Nah, she don't, Kaddy Ko, but I came to see Uncle Slip."

He studied me for a slight second before wrapping me into a playful hug.

"Yo bad ass just not gone stay out the mix, are you? Don't tell Vee I saw you down here, or she might kick my ass," he warned, before tossing a fifty-dollar bill on me.

Of course, I didn't open my mouth after seeing that loot. It had been a nice payday, and the most I'd done was carry some groceries, and pumped a little gas.

Making my way into the first part of the duplex, nine to ten females moved about freely, naked as if all was fair game. I practically had to pick my lip off the floor with how much skin I was able to see in the junkyard through a young teen's eyes.

"Hey, cutie. What can you do with all this?" a brown-skinned stallion asked me, while shaking her backside to the music.

I couldn't say I didn't stare but mesmerized would have been more of the word. Women trailed through the hallways, going back and forth out of rooms, and judging from the dudes lined up in the living room area, they were waiting to pay and play.

Making it through the first side of the house, I cut across to the next room where my uncle was known to relax. Just as I hit the doorway, a cloud of smoke hit my nostrils. Prince's, "Purple Rain" was jamming through the karaoke machine.

"Can I help you, lil homie?" the gunman at the door asked with his head tilted.

"I'm here for my uncle?" I stood there patiently like my face card was platinum in the spot.

Watching him walk over to a large circle gambling table, the guard said a few words, and my uncle's head came rising over everyone that sat around him. He parted from the table and approached me. At twenty-five, he had more paper, and flavor than any nigga, hustler, or pimp in the state or Georgia. He was dressed in a long-sleeve, Versace button-down, a pair of black slacks, and white leather penny loafers. A white, and black mink was laying on his shoulders gently as if his swag was ready to fly away. He was truly a mentor by heart when it came down to being the ultimate hustler of our family.

"Nephew, what you doing around this way without alerting me? You do know it's dangerous out there alone, right?" he asked, pulling on the rolled weed.

Before I could answer, I watched two women enter the room, dropping their daily quota in his palms. They both placed a kiss on his cheek and dispersed, before he turned his attention back to me.

"I know, Unc, I just wanna move like you, man. I want money too, and I can't get that laying around the crib." I tossed my hands in the air.

I noticed all my uncle's shooters and workers moved on one accord, which meant to his beat only. He had more than structure. He had discipline, and with that discipline, brought forth one of the most loyal teams he could've ever put together.

"All you gotta remember is to make the money, Smokey. Don't let it make you. We spend money, money doesn't spend us, so treat it like you own it, cause that's damn sho the only way you gone keep it.

I couldn't do anything but suck up the game because it was definitely authentic the way he was paving it out for me. Still, I wanted my own path, to say I didn't wait around for no handout, or beg. Even as a young teen, my own mama didn't know what I had saved, so my Uncle Slip's words was more closure to my ears. In order to rise, stay quiet, and grind for it.

Just when I was about to reply back to him, a woman's loud scream came from the other side of the building. My uncle gave one nod to his two other associates, Wildman Steve and Earl, and they were up, guns drawn in a blink. These were two guys I knew put fear in the streets when it came down to Slip Rock's word. Killing was more like taking candy from a baby. The ones you didn't want to see smiling on the other side of your door in the middle of the night.

They both moved swiftly through the entrance, closing the door behind them. My uncle was now sitting back in his chair again like all was gravy. The entire room was stiff. After a cool forty-five seconds of silence. Wildman Steve and Earl was pushing a man through the front door by his head. It happened so quick I had to jump back before he landed by me. The top of his skull wore a gash that was running like a faucet. He was grunting, rubbing blood in his eyes, and for a minute I thought he reached up to me for help. I gazed over to my uncle, who still showed no form of empathy for this guy laying beneath his feet.

"So, who is this?" Slip Rock squinted his eyes as if he couldn't see the nigga in front of him.

"A stupid nigga that ain't got no care for living, Lil Slip," Wildman Steve barked, kicking him in the side of his face.

"He was trying to rape one of the girls. I'm guessing his check is running a little late," Earl stepped in with a straight face.

The broke nigga coughed up a little blood, begging to be heard, but my uncle was tuning him out, due to the Prince bumping through the speakers. He snapped a finger and mumbled to his lyrics, while glaring at him with the look of death.

"Wildman, teach ole boy some manners about toying with our ladies." He smiled like *Chucky*, before leaning back in his seat.

Earl, and Wildman instantly began to drag the guy by his arms towards the back door. He kicked his legs, trying to refuse, but a fight did no good. The door closed behind them.

My uncle still grooved around the room like he didn't have a care in the world. That's when I heard a loud gunshot quake from behind the duplex.

Boom!

A few seconds later, Earl came back through the door alone. He returned to his seat, without giving any indication of feelings. All I know is he threw my uncle a thumbs-up, and grabbed his cards to finish off their game of spades. I'm not sure what that meant, but it was like music to Slip Rock's ears. He poured a round of drinks for the table and headed back over to me.

"Nephew, I think it's about time you make it on to the house. Tell Vee I'll be through there tomorrow and see you." He gave me a few dollars, escorting me towards the front door.

"Why can't I just stay here with you and earn some? I can't make nothing sitting in the house," I informed him on my aggravation.

"In due time, neph. In due time. Just not yet." he said, truthfully knowing I was eager to put in that work.

Even though I felt my life was meant to be a hustler, I still respected and valued the older professional's opinion. *My time will eventually come*, I thought as I shot my uncle the deuces before walking out.

The one thing I did know, the city of Atlanta was in for a true money maker. Money that would stamp my name in the dirt of Fulton County.

Chris Green

Chapter 4

Bear Cat

After checking in on two of my new work spots, I decided to drop in over on the south side to see how good the movement was flowing. From the top of Campbellton Road, down to the bottom of Ashby Street, and Simpson Road. I was the man you needed to see if distribution had anything to do with your daily activities around our way. Of course, you had killers like Guy and Pearl around the way, but when it came down to Bear Cat's name ringing bells, let's just say Freaknik was like my welcome home party. I was more than life to the streets. I was the air you needed to survive when it came to the dope game.

Turning my black 1984 Charger on Dill Avenue. I spotted a young face that looked all too familiar. I started to slow down, and when I got closer, I noticed it was lil Smokey. Vee's son. Back in the day I use to try and holler, but of course I know when to step back after Miami T claimed his woman. He was just a man, that fools didn't want to go against. Even after a small dispute, I settled differences with him just to remove the bad blood out the air. Pulling in closer to the sidewalk. I rolled down my passenger window.

"Aye, young blood? Why you sliding around so late? I know Victoria would have a heart attack if she knew what was going on."

Lil man stopped and gave me a look that said, *keep driving*, but I know he was wondering how the hell I was calling his mother's first name as if we were best friends.

"I don't know you, and how you know my mama's name, 'cause I ain't never seen you before?" He looked me up and down, trying to feel my energy.

Killing the engine real quick, I hopped out and leaned against my car. The streetlight above us flickered on just before I started to speak.

"You doing all this walking, you probably ain't even got no reason for being out here. How old are you now?"

"Old enough," he shot back quicker than I expected.

"That's right. I can dig it, young blood." I rubbed my goatee with a smile. "But I'm not your enemy, I swear. I'm actually a good friend of your mama and dad."

"How do I know that?"

"'Cause I wouldn't be standing here saying it, Smokey. I know you move up and down the block daily, more than any average young thug. What you got going for yourself?" I sparked up a Black & Mild, waiting for his response.

"I'm just having fun, making me a dollar or two. I wanna be rich, and that ain't gone come sitting in the house." He smirked, looking up into my Cartier frames.

"That's true, but you gotta know the rules to getting money also, lil one. See, the game is different now. Niggas ain't respecting another man's hustle, knocking theirs in the dirt. That shit makes a dog-eat-dog world, and that's the first way a true money-getter lose. Greed. Rule number one, make your money, but don't try to stick every dollar in your pockets," I warned, flashing him a fan of crispy hundreds.

"It looks like you got all the money in yo pocket. How can I get it like that?" Smokey asked, now giving me his full attention. His brown eyes locked in on the dough and it showed me his deep ambition for chasing it. It reminded me much of myself, and I knew how hard it was to quit once you've started. What else could you do for a young kid with drive to get paper? I did what any other OG would do, I birthed a legend. Digging in my coat, I tossed him a small package. "That's how we getting it round here, lil Smokey. You know what that is?" I studied his face to see his reaction.

"Looks familiar. How do I sell it?"

"Blue bags are five. Yellow bags are ten. Green bags are twenty. We don't do loans, and we ain't bringing nothing but an empty bag home. That's the key to the city right there, lil bro. You gotta move smoove though. I see you all the time sliding around to make your way however you can, but this is a different league. I know your dad, Miami, so I would automatically be dead even introducing that to your hands if he was around to see this. But I also refuse to leave his kid looking for guidance from another dumb fool, just to crash out."

"I can do it. I can do anything if it comes down to business."

I knew he was being overconfident, but for some strange reason, I believed the lil nigga. Slip Rock was already locking in with me on territory, and numbers was gonna rise if we kept our competitors at bay. Little did I know, that was Smokey's whole position. He was a key that opened up the block for us to never look back. One that would earn him a hood rep in Atlanta for the future generations to have it all.

* * *

Venetian Hills Apartments SW Atlanta

Smokey

4 months later

It was more than beautiful outside today. The sun was shining high. People was out and about, and I had made over a thousand bucks this morning, and it wasn't even past twelve in the afternoon. After my run-in with Bear Cat a few months ago, he gave me a start I could never turn away from. I was the youngest hustler in the SWATS, but my respect level was on triple OG, just on the strength of my dad's work that was put in. I moved through my own set of apartments. Served everything, coming from Greenbriar to East Point, and now my name was starting to set in the mud. The ropes were so easy to learn, the rest fell right into your palms to control.

"Ay, Smokey. I got eight, trap baby. Bless me," one of the users asked me out loud.

Placing a yellow bag in his hand, I held up a finger. "No more shorts, old school. I need it all, if you tryna smoke and ball."

"Sho'nuff, trap baby, I got chu, fa'sho." He scurried off, while telling me what I wanted to hear.

I was the master of letting someone kill themselves with business. If you didn't pay me, I cut all dealings. It's just the way the operation went.

The sound of loud music bumping made me turn my head, to see a money-green Monte Carlo flushing down the hill. The car came to a halt directly beside me. A cloud of smoke flushed from the window, and Guy stuck his head out, shooting daggers at me. His lips curled like a snake, and I could tell he wasn't about to say nothing nice.

"Any reason you on my turf, lil boy? This me and Big Pearl shit if you ain't heard. I wouldn't recommend to have any operations going on, if yo people ain't tryna see shit get messy." He flashed a chrome pistol, resting it on the side of his door.

I wanted to run, but I definitely couldn't beat out a bullet, and all I pondered on was the sneaky nigga tryna step out the car, before I even had a chance to make a run for it.

"No problem. I was just passing through," I lied, trying to walk off.

Of course, his associate leaned off the brakes, so the car could roll directly beside me. I still tried to keep my head straight as if I didn't see them.

"Don't look like somebody that pass through here on the normal. What ya holding?"

Right when he asked that question, two all-black Jeep Cherokees came to a screeching stop in front of me, and Guy's car. My uncle Slip Rock jumped out first with a machine gun in hand. Two of his workers, and Bear Cat rose from the opposite vehicle pushing right behind him.

"Smokey, get in the car. . . Ay Guy, is there a problem or some with my nephew? I'm sure if there is, we can handle this cordially." He gripped the gun with two hands.

"Nah, no problem at all, Slip. It's never a problem when it comes to you and Bear Cat. Just try and keep ya peeps outta my money pool, pimping," he addressed before smashing out of the apartments.

Uncle Slip Rock turned to me with anger flushing through his pupils. Anger that let me know I had obviously done something wrong.

"Smokey, what the hell are you doing in these apartments? You're not supposed to be out here." He shoved me into the backseat of a Jeep.

"I didn't know. I only come on the weekends to make the extra money from the high school kids. That's all," I admitted truthfully.

"Smokey, all that's understood, nephew. But we have tricks and plays to this game you have yet to understand.

Trembling around in another person's territory can get you killed, boy. Luckily, I have people all over this place to tell me what's going on, or I would probably have to tell your mother I'm burying her son today," he fumed as we drove out of the apartments.

It didn't take long to arrive back at my mama's house, and Slip forced me to stay in the car, until he explained what happened to his sister. Word for word. He damn sure didn't want the word getting back to my dad, so clearing the air was the only thing on his mind.

Bear Cat turned around in the passenger seat, facing me with a smile.

"I can't say I'm mad at you like Slip, Smokey, but you gotta know your protection is the first thing on our minds while we out'chea fucking around with these felonies. You the youngest, and nobody will be able to sleep well if you got hurt. I mean that literally." I could see the sincerity in his face as he spoke, even though I didn't fully grasp everything he was spitting to me.

"If it's so easy to get money, why do everyone make it so hard for me when I try?" I asked him, truly wanting to know why I kept catching the bad end of the stick.

Huffing, he shook his head, and gave me the realest advice I would ever hear in my life.

"If it was so easy, lil Smokey, everybody would have dough. We fight and work so hard to get it but throw it away freely on shit that values at nothing. The moment when motherfuckers let the money rise higher than life. It became the root of all evil till the end of time. It's just human nature to want more. Some just don't know when to say it's enough.

I sat humbly listening to every word, and it knew it was nothing but pure facts. I was only in the grounding stages of grinding, but I was learning quicker than fast with my do's, and don'ts.

Watching my uncle Slip Rock walk out of my mama's crib. He headed back for the car, opening the back door for me to step out.

"Whatever you do, don't tell her about the drugs," he mumbled just above a whisper, then waved me over to my mother like I was the most honest teen of the year.

I noticed her standing in the doorway waiting for me, and immediately caught the bubble guts. Doing wrong in her eyes was something she didn't see in me, and that was the light I needed her to keep me shaded under.

"So, tell me what happened?" She was tapping her foot fast as a bunny.

I walked towards the stairs for my room, remaining quiet.

"Smokey, your ears must be broke, boy. I said, what happened? Your uncle said someone had a gun." She answered her own question, knowing I wouldn't dare repeat it.

"I'm okay, Mama. A man had a gun, but he wasn't trying to hurt me."

"I wouldn't give a damn. Anybody could have been a subject to violence out there at that moment. How many times do I have to tell you, I don't want you out there on them streets, Smokey?"

"But if I don't be out there, how can I take care of you, and everyone else?"

"That's something you gotta let God worry about cause you just can't do that. I'm obliged to take care of you, but try and make sure I can keep my son, please?"

"I hear you, Mama. I'ma still take care of you," I mumbled, as I turned around to head upstairs.

The one thing I knew, the dope game was more than sweet. It was a chase for whoever's cash played the hustle the best, and I was tryna prove my status could be victorious. I dreamed money, and it was flowing fast like the blood through my fingers. My mind was ready to skip working and was thinking of buying. I knew I wanted to be my own boss, and all I needed was the right amount of money to talk for me. I didn't know how it would be executed, but I damn sho had the start of a plan from that day on.

Chapter 5

Bear Cat

Auto Body Shop

Lee Street, SW Atlanta, GA

2 months later

As I sat in the A/C of my new black '85 Lexus. I put the blunt of Optimo in my hand out in the ashtray, as my lil young Filipino chick tightened me up on some head in the passenger seat. Lil mama was handling that business, and I was damn near at the point where I was ready to go ahead and catch mines, but it felt damn too good. In reality, it was a moment for me to tighten up, instead of lounging around, indulging with bullshit in the mix of work.

It was always the first distraction. I had Smokey serving out the auto shop management office. All the customers had to do was walk in, handle business, and leave back out as if they'd ordered a tune-up for next week.

My phone buzzing broke my fun hour, and I was always forced to answer that jack.

"Yo, wat up?" My ear was up to the receiver, trying to hear the opposite side of my line.

"You're dead, Cat. You, Slip, and all the rest of ya. That's on God, boy," a voice barked through my line, before hanging up.

"What the fuck?"

I brushed shawty off me and fixed my khaki's. Just when I was about to step out of the car, a swarm of police cruisers flooded the parking lot. Easing down in the seat, I pulled lil mama down with me as I watched them raid the spot. The only thing I could think about was Lil Smoke.

* * *

Smokey

Sitting at the desk in Bear Cat's office. I finished bagging up the last ounce of product and started to sack it up in individual Ziploc's to sell. The past few weeks, I was taught everything a man was to know about pushing small packs and holding traps. We had been at it for about two hours and was capping them extra side dollars like the drop was mine. I was trapper of the year if you asked me, and we hadn't even been at it for a whole three-sixty-five.

The front glass doorbell sounded making me look up, but I had yet to see anyone enter. By the time I glanced down to my objective, and back up at the door, the county sheriffs were running through my personal space with guns bigger than me.

"Get the fuck on the ground, nowww!" I heard a voice that sounded a little too light to be black.

I didn't hesitate to get on the ground out of fear of the police firing, but when I thought twice about the loud ass dog I heard barking, I shot for the open window five feet away from me. I didn't know how I was gonna land, but I did know it wasn't that much of a fall. Sprinting quickly as I could, I dived out the window and landed directly on my shoulder, against the concrete. It only broke my stop for a perfect comeback. I was up on my feet, getting it like the hundred-yard dash was on the line.

As I headed for the chicken wire fence behind the building, I spotted Bear Cat's car smashing out of the parking lot.

It's like he didn't move until he saw me leave out of that auto shop.

Using my hood skills, I climbed the twelve-foot gate with ease and jumped clean over. My feet were once again gliding across the pavement like Speedy Gonzalez, and the few cops that noticed me were being left in my rear. I wasn't trying to look back, and I damn sure wasn't about to stop, and see if they were still behind me. I was dark-skinned with curly hair, so the heat from the sun instantly began to drench my outfit.

Throwing the drugs I had across the field of grass, I ended up on Beecher Street, coming out on the side of a yellow house. Bear Cat's car slung directly in front of me and mashed the brakes. I nearly pissed in my pants until I noticed he was waving for me to get in.

Running around to the backseat, I jumped inside, and he smashed off, heading back for Cascade Road.

"Damn, lil nigga, you can run. I just knew you wasn't gonna make it outta there. You ain't hurt, is ya?" He cheesed, rubbing my head, while doing eighty miles down a one-way street.

"I'm good, I don't think I like running from cops though." I took a deep breath, slumping down in the seat.

Bear Cat whipped the car like a pro down a few back streets, and before you know it, we were on the west side of Atlanta, coming down Martin Luther King. It didn't take long before we pulled up to Harris Point off Simpson, and headed into a small, two-bedroom apartment.

I was looking at the woman who was opening the burglar bar door and noticed how gorgeous she was. She had a healthy body, long hair and brown eyes, and chunky cheek bones. She had some backside, but petite in the waist. Bear

Cat didn't usually keep a stranger with him, so I figured she had to be his girlfriend.

Getting inside, he crashed on the couch, and I took a seat beside him.

"Good job, Smokey. I'm proud of how you handled yaself, because I can't give bad news without my head being ripped off in the process. This for you." He slapped fifteen hundred dollars on my chest. I started moving them bills and seeing all hundreds. That's all it took to turn me out.

"This? Just for running from the cops?" I asked to make sure it was all mine.

"No, that's for moving like you wanna keep your freedom and this movement. Ya pops a be proud of ya."

Stuffing it in my pocket, I looked up at the curious grown woman staring at me like a zombie. All her clothes were tight, showing her curves, and she stood there quiet like she was about to recite a speech.

"Oh, I forgot, Lil Smoke. This is Marcy, my friend. Marcy, this lil nephew Smokey. Vee's son." He grinned like he was my dad.

"I know who son he is. His lil cute ass. You got this young ass boy risking his life in the auto shop when you could have had him here, and just worked the burglar bar door, dumb-dumb. I do more traffic than that bomb ass shop," she boasted truthfully to him.

He jumped up like that was the most spectacular idea ever, because he was back to pulling packs out his jacket, dropping 'em on her table. "That's smart as fuck, Lil Smokey a catch all the love on the westside, just from yo daddy's name. Niggas will break they neck to come shop, just to be in good graces with T. I mean, that's if you up to making the paper?" he asked as if I didn't want to take the job.

I gazed at the drugs and thought about all the money I had been earning. *Fuck it, why not take a rise up*? I just didn't know it was a decision I made too fast, until it was too late.

Going under the sofa, Bear cat pulled out a small .380 handgun. Handing it to me, he spoke sternly, "Don't pull it, unless you about use it, and if you don't use it when you pull it, you gone wish like hell you had. Ya understand me?"

"Yeah, Bear Cat, I'm not a rookie. I should be okay." I tucked it neatly under a pillow.

"My man." He chuckled. "Look, Marcy is good people, she'll take care of you if you need anything, so you ain't gotta budge from your post. She'll grow on you, trust me." He headed for the door, leaving out.

The small walls of the apartment were decorated with photos, and plants. Not luxury, but clean enough to sleep. I sat the supply in front of me, preparing for what I had to do and Marcy came, sitting down close beside me.

"How old are you?" She was close to me, breathing like she needed to know.

"I'm thirteen." I tried to slow my heart down, exhaling.

She rubbed across my pants slowly, grinning like a villain.

"Just get comfortable, lil king. You ain't gotta worry 'bout nun, when you with me." Her tone was sweet and assuring, like Sade.

All I could do was nod as she moved over to the door, applying the locks.

Chris Green

Chapter 6

Ms. Vee

I was moving around my home, cleaning with a purpose. My mind was trying to place things together to move my family away for the better. All I needed was the right plan, and to start networking in order to see a difference, because the hood in the West End was becoming more than terrible. Smokey was starting to stay out in the streets more, and the rest of my kids only looked up to him for advice and all the choices for them to make.

We were living almost nine deep in a home, and my husband was nowhere to control the same mess he started. I shared my home with Linda and her kids because T's children were just like mine. We shared that much of a strong bond. I was respectable and knew how to play my part as a woman, regardless of any game being run. My only priorities were to take care of the kids, and stay down until his next year or so, ticked down to come home. Stress with everything else wasn't even a factor.

"Mama, Daddy on the phone." VeeBee, stepped into the living room, handed me the cordless hook.

"Thank you, baby." After she departed, I placed my ear up to the line. "Hello?"

"My queen, how you?" T's voice sounded off coolly, making me smile.

"Hey, boy. No call in three days, you must want a divorce?" I smacked my teeth, knowing I was happy like hell to hear from him.

"Nah, love. Never that, I been working, that's all. Nothing means more than family, Vee. Don't play with me."

"I know, T. Have you been okay, or is there anything I need to do?" I asked, as Linda walked out the front door with the kids.

"Yeah, there kinda is, Vee. You know I'm crazy about you, and the kids being protected. I can't always have eyes on the streets, but it's time to start making arrangements for you, and the fam."

I listened to him talk, and I could sense more was wrong. T was never a man to worry, so when he did, shit was definitely out of place.

"Baby, you're scaring me," I voiced in a serious tone. "What's going on?"

It was a couple seconds of silence, before he spoke.

"A beef I had back in the day. I think a few people may be out looking for me. I'm not sure, but we can never be too careful. The name I told you a while back, he's up there, according to a few of my close friends down in Florida. Now I know you ain't going for nothing strange, ma, but these are some different type of individuals. They have no feelings. So, from today on, I need you to keep Smokey, OJ, and the girls around you at all times. Where is he, anyway?" He questioned.

"T, Smokey acts like your ass one hundred percent. His black self is arrogant, smelling himself, and I'm starting to think he wants to be you reincarnated. I don't know what he's doing anymore."

"He's just trying to do what he see, Vee. That boy has been in love with money since he was able to know what it is and does. He's tryna grow up and learn responsibilities. I did at the same age. You have to just keep an eye on him, and watch from a distance, because he's gonna have to start helping you out soon."

I paced around quietly with the phone, listening with one ear, even though it was going out the other. I would never willingly consent to my son being a product of our environment. We had already suffered, and money didn't mean shit, if it wasn't family around to enjoy it with.

"T, I'm not letting Smokey ass breathe, unless I know the oxygen he sucking in is clean. He's our son, not a field worker, and he's only thirteen," I stressed.

"But he's also a man, and he's gonna find it, if you try and hide it. Listen, Vee, I know our boy is growing, but he ain't a baby anymore. Let him learn from mistakes and take the consequences like a man. It's the only way he will start to make better choices. He's gonna be the leader of our family one day. Let him begin his journey."

Even though I didn't want to hear it, I accepted T's request and remained quiet. "I hear you. I'll try. That's all I can do."

"And that's why I love you. Stay focused. Kiss the fam and let all my babies know I cherish them all."

Sure thing, King." I blew a kiss into the line, hanging up.

Taking a seat at the kitchen table, I thought about Smokey, knowing he was bound to fall victim soon to some bull. All that smelled so good in the beginning, usually turned to shit when you had one foot in the door, and one foot out. I knew I didn't want him taking the same route as T, to survive or make a name. I just wanted my son achieving and building whatever he thought was necessary for his success. I just didn't want him losing his life in the process.

The back door opening, forced my head to turn around, spotting the devil himself walking in. His head was low, grass was on the back of his jacket, and I could tell from how slow he was walking that tired wasn't a word in his membrane.

"Smokey, where have you been?"

I was hoping he'd tell me the truth, so I'd actually know what the hell was going on with my son so I could help, but that was just all I could do. Hope.

His brown eyes read mine and knew I wasn't gonna let up. He took a seat next to me at the table, folding his arms.

"I hustle, Mama. Everyday. I know that you against it as well, but I like what I do. I don't know why, I just do. I know I'm able to handle myself out there, and I don't like when you worry. I hate to see you in need. I got a dream, Ma, and it ain't wishing to move out the ghetto one day. It's to own it. To do that, we need money. My dad isn't here for the usual pampering everyone loves. But I am."

The shit he just spilled had me lost for words. I wanted to reach over and slap a whole twelfth-grade education into his ass. On another note, I felt every word he said, as if it was repeating back through my ears like a sweet lullaby. It sounded like T was sitting directly in front of me, the day he made a promise to take care of me for life. He had all intentions on keeping that, and it was looking me dead in the eyes at that moment.

Instead of going with my first comment, I gathered my thoughts and cleared my head.

"I love you, Smokey, and I know this world just ain't big enough for people like you, and yo daddy. I'm gonna tell you like I told him." I pointed a finger, my lips trembled with shakiness 'cause I wanted to cry, but I stood firmly.

"You live a life and I hope you know pain comes with it. I better know where you are at all times. I don't give a damn about no trap, cap, nothing. You better come home to me every damn night, and when I tell you to stay in, I don't want you going against it, just to make a dollar. If you gonna make the money, do it smart, and something with it after. I will be your new accountant, so break ya pockets," I ordered with my hand out.

I knew he was on some bullshit when he got to grinning and digging. He came out his pants with so many bills, I damn near had to do a double take. I knew I counted a cool fifteen hundred just off eyeballing it. Picking it all up, I gazed down at his black ass curiously.

"What the hell you been selling?" I asked after flipping through it a tad.

He burst out laughing, trying to skate from the table."
"Nah, Ma, that question was never in the deal."

"Deal, my ass. Nigga, you got car fare, and enough to buy a year worth of insurance." I shook my head, but damn sure couldn't be disappointed.

"I just wanta keep some in my bank for ya, Mama. It's ain't nothing." He smiled.

Reaching in my pocket for the new beeper I just picked up, I tossed it over. "That's your new lifeline. Keep it at all times. Like ya second pair of skin."

"I got chu, Ma." He kissed my cheek before disappearing upstairs.

After making sure he was gone, I started back my count, and after my number reached four thousand, I folded the rest back up, and decided to mind my own damn business. I always played smart not hard, but as long as my child needed me for backing, he had my assistance for eternity. My eyes closed, and the thought of T stepping out of those walls soon shot tingles in my heart. Until that time, I was planted in the mud, waiting for our royal family to be united.

Chris Green

Chapter 7

Marcy's Spot, Westside of Atlanta

Smokey

Sunlight boomed heavy through Marcy's apartment, and I was just breaking down my second package of the day. Crack was really the hypnosis on medal, so that shit mixed with the heat only made the fiends geek harder and sweat a little extra. Marcy's shit was like a drive thru at Wendy's, except you wasn't eating none out this spot. I had whites, blacks, Asians, and even a few Africans pulling up to spend some dough on my dad's cause.

Marcy walked into the kitchen wearing a tall white shirt, and pair of footie socks. Of course, she was smiling like hell but her beauty, mixed with kindness, is what allowed me to relax more with her. She showed interest in me the first few weeks I was here but made her claim not too long after. At thirteen, it was hard to say I knew what to do with a grown woman, but she surely knew what to do with me. After my light shyness wore over the first few times, I became more accustomed, confident. She was mine whenever present, but I wasn't making myself comfortable under Bear Cat's business.

"I see you don't like to stay in a bed," her tone was sarcastic

I chuckled, splitting down the four-way of dope in front of me. Separating a few quarters, and halves, I started to form me up a few gram bags. "That bed ain't going nowhere. This money will split on us." I winked at her, rocking back and forth in front of me.

"I won't split on you. With money, or without it," she mumbled with a nod.

"Oh yeah? How do I know you will though, Marcy? We wouldn't even be right here if it wasn't for this." I had my hands up in surrender, knowing she might take it offensive.

She sat down at the table with me, clearing her throat. "Smokey, I'm not sure how many girls you've dealt with in your lifetime, But I'm older, and different. I never asked to be ya girl or woman, from these circumstances, but you've been the only side I stood next to in the past month. I rock and respect you 'cause you know how to treat me. It's rules to love also, but I've passed on my share. Now I just stop where I like. That was until I met you." She threw in the remark, confusing me.

"So how long did you plan on having this stop with me?"

Blushing, she stood up, knowing her backside was nearly coming from underneath her shirt. "That's the key baby. "There's nothing else to like past this ride. Malfunction on stuck mode I should say." She blew a kiss, just as her doorbell buzzed.

I started to get back on my task when she departed, but the quietness in the spot after the first two minutes, sent chills up my back. At first, I thought she served a customer and sent him on by his way, but then my sight touched the family room. Four cops stood in the house, with Marcy in a pair of cuffs. I was regretting ever moving, and right as I tried to back up into the kitchen, all eyes shot over to me.

"Freeze!" was all I heard before dashing out of the back door. I took off up the sidewalk, running like a free slave. The next thing I saw was sunshine and blue skies, but it damn sho wasn't going away. Dizziness circled my eyes when I hit the ground, and a buff police officer that looked like Mario Lopez from Saved by the Bell. "Hey there, buddy,

I didn't hurt you too bad, did I?" He was waving a hand in my face trying to shake me back to reality.

After five minutes of hyperventilating on the ground, the officer sat me in the backseat of a cruiser in cuffs. My mama had already been alerted, and Marcy was having a mental breakdown thirty feet away from me. I watched a group of investigation units walking out the apartment with large Hefty garbage bags of weed by the load. Everyone was standing outside, with the scopes on, and if my mama wasn't able to get me out of this, I was probably about to be shredded underneath this entire mayhem.

Officer Mario Lopez, climbed back into the front seat, started typing on a laptop. That alone started to rumble my stomach.

"Excuse me, sir, would you mind telling me what's going on?

He glanced back at me with one of those friendly neighbor ass smiles.

"Morning, chief. I'm surprised you don't remember nothing. Uh, apparently, you were caught fleeing an apartment that's been under surveillance. You got caught with a load man. Drugs, and stuff. You wanna talk about it?" he asked me with a shrug like, it was a cool day to chat.

The line sounded as if a mouse had written it personally, and I wasn't about to say shit to nobody about who, what, when, and where. I sat back against the seat, slowly lowering my head.

"Nah, I'll try, and sit back to recollect a minute."

"Suit yourself, but hey, you're only thirteen. I mean, I can't say I remember pacing someone your age at these type of scenes. I wouldn't suggest you throw yo life away for somebody that's ready to see you take the fall."

I dismissed buddy's whole convo, especially when I spotted my mama's car pulling in like a bat out of hell. The most I could see was her hopping out and questioning the first officer spotted. Marcy just happened to be standing they're against the car when her rampage started. Obviously, she heard the wrong thing, 'cause she looked at them both a lil crazy before grabbing Marcy by the head. Within seconds, she had the cops trying to stop her own case from transpiring at the moment.

"Aye, man, check on my moms and let her know I'm okay. You see she panicking." I tried to get him to assist, instead of sitting there.

He popped his gums, but still did what I asked, and retrieved my mom. I watched as he pointed over to the cruiser I was sitting in and brought her over.

"Smokey, are you okay, baby?" She rushed to the bars, locking onto my fingers as if life was just over.

"Yeah, yeah, Mama. I want you to calm down though. I don't need you stressing. We already talked about this."

"Smokey, this isn't a minor joke, honey. That shit you got caught up with is about to bring a world of shit down on us. I can't just walk you away from this. These white people ain't gone let this go," she mumbled, so only I could hear.

I didn't want to go through the back and forth in front of the authority, so I played my role well.

"Just see if they will let you come down to the station and sign me out until I see the court. It's worth a try. Both of us can't be down, so someone has to stay confident. Please, Mama." I needed her to know how serious it was, there was no idea of how it all ended. I was still young and wanted to explore way more with my life. Bear Cat wouldn't be able to find out until he reached back on this side of town. I was stuck, but I knew one thing was for sure. I was staying solid to do what I did so far. Master the hustle.

"I will, just stay quiet, and we about to ride the wheels off. You gotta slow down, Smokey." She rubbed my neat hair though the bars, then turned around to speak with the officer.

That didn't last too long. She looked at me once more, before getting in her car to leave.

When the escorting man got back in the driver seat. He said six words to me that soiled my day.

"Looks like you're riding with me."

After that, I closed my eyes, waiting until I reached my new destination for the moment.

***

It had been two weeks since I gotten booked, and I couldn't say it was a good feeling. Since I was so young, with a top priority case as a juvenile, I was bounded over to Jefferson Street, the County Jail. I was charged as an adult and forced to stay behind the wall, until a court date was set for a judge to view my situation. I was only thirteen, and fighting a drug bust the state of Georgia had seen with a minor. I wasn't prepared to deal with how hard shit was coming at me, but at the moment I had no choice.

Hearing the cell tank open, the sheriff stood in front of me with a pair of cuffs, ready to put on my wrists. I let him put em on, just to try, and get some closure to the situation.

Walking out on the courtroom floor, the first person I spotted was my mama sitting the first pew. She blew a kiss and her smile put me at ease.

Two more bailiffs entered the room, guarding the doors, and the back seats were filled with a few citizens of Fulton

County. They sat me in the seat, next to a fake lawyer dressed in a cheap suit. His smile said things maybe had a chance to turn out good, but his eyes said he clearly couldn't be trusted.

"Who are you?" I asked, trying to read the papers on the table in front of us.

"I'm your public defender. I just need you to be quiet, and all will go well," he replied with a pat on my shoulder, like we were just best buddies.

The judge entered the courtroom, sitting in his chair. Everybody formed at attention. His face was all pale with small green eyes. Fat guy could easily go for Santa Claus.

"I wanna clear the air on something this morning, before we began on this specific case. I, Judge Tom Dillon the first, have never witnessed something like this as a judicial system official. Is there any legal guardians present for this defendant?"

I watched my mama stand up with her hand raised.

"Me, I'm his mother."

"Ma'am, I'm gonna be honest with you. It's sad to say that a child is possible to fall into a pothole so steep. Never in life has something been so disturbing to my mental, as a father, a parent. One that truly commits time with raising their seeds for success, or straight path. I'm sorry to say that I don't see that revolving around this household, Ms. Carter."

He was looking at my mama with a distasteful mug, like she was just a villain. I knew she was about to go from zero to one hundred from the way her face started to crunch up. It didn't take much for her to blow a fit, and it wouldn't do anything but mash me into a deeper can.

"Excuse me, what the hell is that supposed to mean? I'm doing the best with my child as far with raising him, but as far as you disrespecting my parenthood with your lil fancy ass words is not gonna work on me."

"Ma'am, your son was caught with enough drugs to start his own empire. Numerous of different narcotics. It's kind of hard for me to see that you're raising a child, not a kingpin. At thirteen years old, he's involved with things that a child would have to be introduced into. These things make you an unfit mother, Ms. Carter, and that's just pathetic."

Hey, man, you don't talk to my mama like that! Fuck you." I jumped out of my chair with the cuffs shaking wildly.

A few guards came to stand by my side and calm me. One grabbed my arm, while I burned a hole through the white man's pupils. It was common for racist slurs to be thrown when you were dealing with people of the justice system, but I refused to let my mama suffer the torment of embarrassment because of my actions. I knew at that moment, my life as a child was officially over.

"Son, I can understand your frustration, but the law is law. You were bound over from a juvenile facility because of the grade of your charges. Today, your defender has placed you in for a non-negotiable plea to accept, where we can get this case out of my courtroom. Is this understood between the defendant, and the state?"

"Yes, Your Honor, crystal," the district attorney nodded with joy.

My public defender, rose to his feet with a few papers in his palms. "Yes, Judge Dillon. We are prepared to take the non-negotiable plea to ensure my client gets a second chance, being that he's only a child."

The silence the judge gave triggered my nervousness a little more, before he removed his glasses to speak. "He's gonna receive a chance to redeem his life and actions, Mr. Pollock, but I'm afraid that it won't be until he serves his time for the crime committed. My ruling is eight, to serve four in a youth detention center. A few drug classes, and of course, anger management. If that's all surrounding the case plan, we can rule on it, and move to the next."

"We are willing to accept, Your Honor," my public pretender answered quickly for me.

"Eight what? My son is a just a baby. He's never been arrested his entire life. You can't just send him away like this. It has to be a higher authority," my mama questioned with pain eating through her voice.

"No, there isn't, ma'am. This is the higher authority, and your son has to stand for the crime he's committed. It's better than having your child committed to the state, Ms. Carter. I know you care, but you have to allow him free will to stand for his own actions, and not cover him to the point where it could fall back on you. This is for his own good," Judge Dillon explained before looking back at me.

I glanced back at my mama, and when she nodded confirmation for me to comply, and she was the only one standing in that room at the moment I wasn't going against.

Taking the pen from my fake lawyer's hand. I signed my name on the paper.

When the sheriff came to lead me back to the cell tank, I blew my mother a kiss and walked through the door to my new life. It was day I'd never forget. One that made me the man I was in the future. I was stepping in the system a boy, but I was damn sho coming back out a man.

Chapter 8

Milledgeville YDC Detention Center

I got back to the center and was placed back into the dormitory immediately. My anger was so built up I couldn't do nothing but catch the first chair I saw, taking a seat. I stared up at the boring movie they aired on the TV and instantly thought about my mama, brothers, and sisters. The past few months I had been away from them started to show me something so valuable. At your darkest, hurtful, lonely nights, you would miss all the things, that seemed like they were so easy to keep. I never knew the struggle of doing jail time in juvie, would make you regret trying to dance anywhere near some drugs.

I had it bad at heart, 'cause my reality still felt like I was supposed to be out there getting to the grind. It was just my one fetish that couldn't be broken, having an undeniable love for that paper.

I felt someone poking me on the shoulder roughly, forcing me to turn my head. When I spotted the three boys standing behind me, my mind went blank on their reason for approaching.

"Uh, am I missing something?" I gazed at them all, confusion burning a hole through my temple.

One of the boys, obviously leading the other two, stepped forward and smirked. His eyes were like a snake, low and wide, and every time he spoke, his ears would poke out to the side. He was the only kid in YDC that knew for a fact he was never going home. We never had a run-in before on bad terms, I guess, until that moment.

"Smokey from the SWATS. They say yo folks rich out there on the streets. How 'bout you pay for our snacks next weekend, and get my girl down here to visitation? Yo folks don't mind, do it?" He mugged, folding his arms, like I was just soft or some shit.

"Listen, man. I'm not trying to have any problems with you, Laro." I called him by his nickname to try an ease the tension.

"Nahhhh, see, I ain't been feeling this shit today, so I need some extracurricular activities to place my attention on. It's free pick Tuesday, nigga." His finger tapped the side of my head this time.

Before I could even gather my second thought, I was landing a hard right fist into this nigga's jaw. I could hear it crack like the sound of a dustpan slamming across a counter. I saw the dizziness in his eyes, and just as his head collapsed against the day room floor, the other two boys were on my ass like white on rice. They were jumping me of course, and I tried my best to handle the business. As I fought for my life, Laro happened to get back up, and it was all hell.

Three fools were raining fists down on me like a faucet, and the rest of the teens were standing around watching me go through the mud with these three idiots. Just when I felt myself ready to fall, I spotted one of the dudes flying off me. It gave me enough time to shoot Laro a nasty two-piece, putting him back on the floor. When I got a chance to glance over at my last target, I watched a tall white guy knock his ass out of both shower shoes. He didn't even break a sweat. He looked up at me and nodded.

The C.O.s running inside the dorm, caught my attention next. They wasted no time restraining every inmate involved, throwing us into cuffs. We got pulled out in the hallway and made to face the wall. My mind was really racing now. I was bleeding from the nose, heart pounding like a galloping horse, and I just really witnessed a white boy help me in a brawl against some real hardheads. I really didn't know what the hell to think.

"Inmates moving," a guard yelled, and pulled me forcefully by the cuffs. Before I knew it, I was getting tossed in the hole. Lockdown unit where we only came out once a day, for an hour. The cell they threw me in was slick dirty as hell, and my property was still in the dorm. I took a seat on the cold steel, exhaling from the recent scuffle.

The door's buzzing again, caused me to stand up. After a few seconds it opened, and the white kid involved with our small riot, walked inside. I had to say I was glad to see him, rather than one of those fools I had to beat.

After the officer closed the door. He jumped up on the empty top bunk. "I'm not sure if you even wanted a bunkmate, bro, but I won't be here long. I'm transferring to Eastman tomorrow." He shook his head, looking more exhausted than me.

"What's your name?" I held out my hand.

He accepted my gesture without hesitation.

"They call me White Boy Keith.

"I'm Smokey, from—"

"Atlanta, I know. I heard a little bit about you."

I had to pause when he said that, because usually when someone hears things about an individual, it's either good or bad. "It's not what you think." He chuckled as if he was reading my mind. "I heard about your case, and just know that you're a hustler. It's all through the YDC."

I knew he wasn't lying because I heard the same stories flying around my ears during my stay at the facility. I allowed it to go on, just to keep niggas lost about what actually happened, but in actuality it really didn't matter.

Chris Green

"Yeah, I was into some other stuff out there in the streets. It kinda cost me a little time to sit down," I admitted. "What you here for?"

He wanted to say something but held his tongue. Then he gave me an indirect answer.

"Something similar to you."

Even though I wanted to know more, I respected his blunt response. He was a cool-looking white kid, couldn't have been more than one or two years older than me, if not the same age. His hair was wavy like Justin Timberlake's, and his light bright eyes would trick you into thinking that he didn't have a gangsta, or crooked bone in his body.

"Man, I never thought I would see a white boy that can box like you. Thanks for the help back there, for whatever it's worth." I shook his hand once more.

He laughed, shaking his head at me. "No problem, bro, but I'm not white either. Just light-skinned, fool. I'm black like you. They just call me white, because I'm a little brighter than the usual ghetto people they're used to meeting."

We both had to share a laugh, before it grew silent again. I could see he didn't want to say much, but what was understood didn't have to be explained.

"Hey, man, take my info, maybe we can link when you come home. It's never no telling if we might be on the same thing." He scribbled a number and his name on a piece of paper, before handing it to me.

Folding it up, I tucked it inside of my paperwork. "That's something you don't even have to repeat. I can't say I've met a real one like you, but I can say I'm glad you came at the right time."

I talked to Keith throughout that night until he transferred the following morning. By that time, I had felt we'd known each other forever. I never knew I'd just met a friend who would help me become one of the most known faces in the state of Georgia. A face that would be known as, "The Plug."

Chris Green

Chapter 9

3 years later

Greyhound Station, Atlanta, GA

Smokey

It had been a while since I stepped foot into the free world, and I had to admit it felt great. I maxed out on my juvenile sentence, and I was now coming from behind those gates, a free man. Seventeen with a mean dream. My mama requested to come pick me up, but I chose to maneuver through the city a bit, just to get a feel for the spot again.

After being released from the institution they dropped me off at the nearest Greyhound Station, with twenty dollars in my pocket. The air smelled so different, it was all changed up. The streets looked more vulnerable to my eyes. I watched the live traffic flutter through the lanes of downtown Atlanta and smiled at the new energy I was harboring.

Walking across the small intersection lane, inside the corner store, I headed to the counter and got change for the twenty bucks I had on me. I was moving so fast my property, resting under my arm in a brown bag, ripped and poured out on the floor of the corner store.

"Damn!" I reached down to pick up the mess, and my eyes landed on something I hadn't seen in a long time. Grabbing Keith's number, my mind went to roaming.

"Aye, man, let me get a few quarters to use the payphone." I slid the man a dollar bill back through the money drawer.

Pushing out to the parking lot, I placed a call to the number he left me with back at the detention center. It rung a few times, before the line went silent.

"Who is this?" I heard a voice come alive through the receiver.

"Keith? Is that you?" I asked, not recognizing the tone.

More silence filled the air, then he responded, "Who is this?"

"I was locked up with him a while back in juvenile, I'm his friend, Smokey. I might have the wrong number," I said, preparing to hang up.

"Smokey?" he repeated my name.

"Yeah, this is me," I added, not knowing if I truly had the right person.

"Where are you?"

"I'm down in Garnett Train Station, at the Greyhound. I just got out, man. I just happened to run across yo number, my family don't even know I'm out."

"Stay right there. Don't move," he ordered with more excitement in his tone, before hanging up.

I didn't even get a chance to say okay, but I still posted up, waiting to see why I was put on hold to stand in a store's parking lot. I popped a ginger ale and paced in a few circles, while thinking about the movements I needed to set in place for my arrival back home. It couldn't have been more than twenty-five minutes later when my silent thoughts were broken. The loud music bumping through a set of twelve-inch woofers blared in my ears. My eyes spotted a 1990 teal green 600 Mercedes Benz, sliding in the parking lot as it came to a halt.

Keith jumped out the front seat, fresher than a million bucks dipped in baby powder. He sported an all-black Jordache outfit with a pair of black Bally kicks. A few

Cuban links rested on his neck, and a rose gold submariner Rolex watch sparkled like the sun on his wrist. His hair was combed perfect like Tony Montana's, and all you could smell was money when he hopped out of his whip.

"Smokey?" he spoke, removing the expensive frames over his eyes.

I couldn't help but to smile, seeing my old friend shine like the big man of city. "Wassup, Keith? Long time coming, my man." I embraced him with a handshake, and brotherly hug.

"You, my boy. I'm glad to see you make it back to the other side. Welcome home, my nigga." He tossed twenty grand in my hands, rolled up in hundreds.

It had been a while since I'd seen some paper, so twenty bands had me ready to bust a sweat, thinking the cops might have been watching from a distance. I dropped a few bills and scurried to pick it up.

Keith laughed at me, and I was sure it was because of how nervous I was moving. Hell, who wouldn't move nervous when weighing jail, and the love of money?

"Damn, Keith. What's this? You know you can't just move fast like this, before I get the hang of acting up again." I stuffed it quickly into my pockets.

"That's nothing. Just some pocket change to say something inside of it. We got a big day, man, I been waiting on you long enough. Hop in." He pointed to the passenger seat of his nice ass ride.

I didn't hesitate to catch shotgun, admiring the luxury vehicle. Not too many of these ran through my family, but I was surely about to change that up.

"So, what's it feel like, Smokey?" he asked before pulling out the parking lot.

"Do you mean to be home, or the feeling of what I'm about to try and accomplish?" I replied with a straight face.

Keith nodded quietly, knowing exactly what I meant. Instead of hitting me with the small talk, he fed me the business.

"I'm dealing with you because I trust you, Smokey, so I hope that value is priced high inside of your heart. I don't deal with many, but you're a friend. As long as you keep it thorough, we can always eat. The rest is simple and free. Ya feel me?" He tapped my shoulder to make sure I was listening well.

"I hear ya, Keith. I'm saying is this like the first day of my job internship, or something?" I joked, not thinking much of what he was saying.

"If you're trying to be rocking with me, it is. I need you to have your head straight if I'm bringing you in on what's going on."

When I saw how serious he was, I washed all silliness out my system, and locked in. "You got my attention, I'm down," I confirmed.

"Cool, I wanna show you something." He grinned, jumping on to Interstate 400.

Chapter 10

Po Boy

East Atlanta

I couldn't help but to pull on lil mama's hair while she threw that ass back on me like I wasn't about to handle the business. She was getting wetter by the second, and her amazing body kept me in the house an hour past my usual curfew to be on the streets. She was trying to fuck the soul out a nigga, that's how deep she arched her back. I grabbed onto her waist, trying to punish her sweet spot, and I was nearly on the verge of spilling everything I had in shawty's belly, until the sound of my phone broke my fun time.

"Damn, Po, don't stop, baby," she moaned, sounding better than anything that pierced my ears that day.

Slowing my pace down, I came from in between them legs, agitated as fuck.

"Man, who this?" I answered with aggression.

"Check your fucking tone when you talk to me, boy. If I'm calling, it's for a reason."

I didn't want to argue with her at the moment, so I bit my tongue. "What's going on? I'm kinda in the middle of something."

"A woman can wait, trust me. It's been a long time coming, but he's finally here. He was just released this morning."

Her statement froze me in place. I waited years for the moment to face Smokey, enforce my plan, to proceed with the bigger mission. I waited patiently, spared lives, even cut ties to get close enough. That time was officially here.

"I'm glad to finally hear that. What is it you want to happen from this point on?" I asked her to be clear on what was at hand.

"Find the big lick, then shed yo pain on whomever you choose," she ordered before ending our call.

Breathing lightly, I thought about what I had to set in place. It was time to get payback and more, for everything that happened to my people behind the dirty deeds that had been committed.

Rubbing on lil mama's backside, I smiled thinking about the havoc I was gonna cause. *It was all for the family*, I thought, before I rolled back over and handled the business with my late-night action.

***

Smokey

A nigga couldn't have said they've lived the life, if they hadn't hung with a boss like my best friend, Keith. Fuck balling, he was styling with the game, and within a few hours of being home, he showed me exactly why money didn't mean shit. He also showed me the same reason why it was so important to keep it. You didn't meet the average hustler that sold weight, came up, built connections, and retired richer than Pablo, but you damn sho had a lot of niggas that tried. Since my feet touched the soil, Keith had spoiled me with some of the best designers. The newest Fila gear and kicks, Gucci socks, to the shirts. He was tossing cash out for me like a bank was in his trunk, and I couldn't say I wasn't respecting it. After a good time out, he took me to one of the largest homes I had ever stepped foot inside of.

It had to at least be two acres of land, with grass for days, and a four-car garage. I mean, luxurious wasn't the word. It felt like heaven at home, and I was loving it.

"Where the hell are we?" This look like some *MTV's Cribs* shit." I gazed around as we headed inside the large estate.

Marble tile floors, glass ceilings, statues, to rare paintings. The decor of the home was so laced, you could practically add up a half-million-dollar price tag on all the home property I walked past. I trailed with Keith around a large staircase, that led us to a massive living room. A tall, slim white man stood on the sofa, with a pillow in his hand, popping a bad blonde on the ass with it. Another brunette was busy on the couch, enjoying a rolled joint of Mary Jane. He was wearing a white Versace T-shirt, Hugo Boss Khakis, and a pair of plain dress shoes. Dark Ray Bans sat over his eyes, and he immediately looked up at us when we stepped through the room.

"Keith, didn't know you were stopping home early." He cleared his throat, folding his arms slowly.

"Yeah, Uncle Blue, I had to be up front with my next project. This is what I've been waiting for," Keith replied to him with a slow nod.

I wasn't sure what the hell that meant, but his uncle Blue, stepped down from the couch, and took a seat. His face stern. I didn't know what I had walked into, but I had a feeling it was about to walk right into some business, by how focused the older man became.

"Why are you in my home, son?" He sparked a cigarette, staring into my eyes.

I didn't know what the hell that meant, but I wasn't good with tricks. I kept it real. "Yo nephew brought me here. I'm guessing now it was to meet you."

"What's your name, kid?"

"Smokey."

"Okay, Smokey. First rule. Stop talking so fucking much. I shouldn't have to know why you're in my home. You were brought by family, which means family is responsible. So don't make my family look bad, do you understand?" he stated with ease, like this shit had been written a thousand times. I confirmed to myself my brain was focused and replied cautiously.

"Yes."

"Where are you from, Smokey?" He exhaled a cloud of cancer.

"Atlanta, the SWATS."

"Cool, now you're from Oregon. You've been touring in Atlanta for new real estate, and you're on a six-month business venture. Don't worry about the business, I'll set it up for ya."

"Okay." I looked over at Keith in confusion.

His uncle was now standing, as he nudged out his nicotine bud.

"I'll make this easy for you, Smokey bear. We sell 'em whole like Lowes, but we've also mastered the art of not slipping when ice skating. They go for thirty apiece, we take Twenty-five. Plenty as you can handle, my friend, just remember, slips will make it to where you can never see a blessing again. It's a pleasure to meet you. Let's make money and be family." He flashed a million-dollar smile.

I couldn't believe what I just heard. I hadn't even been at home a full day, and I was already connected with the right man to drop a load off when I touch. It was like God was blessing the dope game to run to me. I wasn't half-stepping with the hustle anymore. I was full throttle. The money light was back on in my head, and Keith's grin solidified my new job that was thrown on the table.

"Let me ask you, Smokey. You did three years, right?" Blue asked while twirling a strand of one of the white bunny's hair.

"Yeah, three."

"That's reasonable for these two headaches right here huh, what do you think?" He tickled between the thighs of the opposite chick this time.

"Excuse me?" I raised an eyebrow, wondering what he was indicating.

"Pussy, Smokey. Go to the back and get some. Me and Keith will be waiting when you're done. It's tradition." He waved his hand, pushing the two beauties towards me.

They both giggled, latching around my waist, like I was a new weight training toy. The petite brunette didn't hesitate to plant a few kisses on my neck, and I was getting excited just from their beauty alone.

I glanced over to Keith's crazy ass for approval, and he quickly shot the deuces, before grabbing the remote for the ninety-inch Panasonic big screen.

"Y'all mind leading the way?" I asked them with a hint of nervousness.

Pulling me by the arms towards the bottom level hallway, they led me to a master bedroom that rested in a space by itself. It was fixed for a king sho nuff, and before I could get through the door good enough, I was being escorted out of my pants. Once the door closed, the rest was history. I didn't know if it was just my luck, or if I had a rabbit's foot in my body. After three years, I came home, and made myself a boss within a few hours.

Chris Green

Chapter 11

Eastside of Atlanta, Kirkwood aka Lil Mexico

Mama Vee

It had been so long since my baby boy stepped foot under my roof, and I was glad the wait was finally over. He was a free man, and nearly the entire family gathered at my home to welcome him back. His brothers and sisters were packed, running through the foyer. Relatives drank and got tipsy. Some sat around eating, but most were anticipating the same thing as me, watching my son walk through that front door. I was located on the east side of Atlanta now, and the fuckery was nearly the same as every other neighborhood, I could think of. I just prayed it was sufficient enough for Smokey to stay out of trouble.

The front door opening broke my train of thoughts, and I screamed to the top of my lungs, watching my baby walk through the door. I jumped in his arms, raining him with smooches, then he gave me a hug.

"We missed you, baby. Surprise." I pinched his cheeks, realizing that he wasn't a baby anymore. He was grown and it showed.

"Welcome home, Smokey!" The family yelled in unison, as I allowed him to breathe.

He was dressed in new clothes, and a rich looking white man was following behind him.

"Thank y'all." He glowed in excitement while hugging everybody. It was a dream to see him bonding with his younger relatives, truly, the whole family. It was hard to keep bondage together, and these were moments that lifted that nasty struggle from above us.

"So, what y'all been up too? Did ya miss me?" He walked around, asking all the silly questions he possibly could.

Instead of breaking his vibe to see where his mind was at, I let him enjoy himself. He partied with a few old friends, chopped it up with a couple older parents that still catered to him since he was a baby. He even had a drink or two, and it was funny to see that, being my son was seventeen now. It was kinda like I didn't even have a say so in my heart.

After an hour of running through the home, linking back with everyone, Smokey and his friend took a seat at my kitchen table with me.

"So, how does it feel to be back?" I asked, knowing he probably couldn't even explain.

"It's like a new life, Ma. I feel refreshed. That little time molded me to be better at what I do, and smarter on when I move from this day on. It showed me a lot. This is where I met my main man Keith right here." He nodded towards his friend.

"I see, now that you two are out and together, what do you plan on doing?"

He paused with his answer, and when he stuttered, I knew it was more behind whatever he's giving me. I allowed him to still think he was running game.

"I'm gonna do what I do best, Mama. Take care of you and the family. I know you hate my actions on what it takes to do it, but I hate the risk of leaving you on this earth without help for my little brothers and sisters. It's all I know." He kept it straight up with me.

Digging into his pocket, he snatched out a bundle of rolls, dropping them on the table in front of me. I frowned, thinking he'd committed the worse, with all the money laying in front of me.

"Where the hell did you get this?"

"Relax, Ma, you ain't gotta stress all that. I can promise you I ain't did nothing crazy. Take that and use it for what you need around here. The extra help will lift some weight off you, and I don't wanna hear anything about now. It's yours." He pushed it closer across the table to me.

Calling for my second oldest, O.J., Smokey asked him to grab the rest of his brothers and sisters. By the time they all piled into the kitchen, Smokey was standing at the head of the table, silently gazing at us all.

"I wanna let all y'all know first off, I love y'all uncondi- tionally. Now that I'm home, there ain't no need for stressing 'bout nothing. I wanna take the Carters to new levels, better thinking, and more places with the ideas I have in mind. I want us to grow, to never have to want. I know I've been away for a minute, a good while actually. I'm here now, and within these next few months, you guys will have anything your heart desires. I just need y'all to trust me and follow my lead."

His statement definitely had my lips sealed. He was now once again the man of the house, and I refused to go against his reasoning for what he was about to do. It was the first stage of our household to regain strength. Listening to avoid the turmoil that laid ahead, Smokey was more than good when it came to bringing nothing to something. He was perfect.

"Everyone has to play a part, only your part, and you'll reap the benefits. O.J., I'm gonna use you as my runner for the community. Just to let me know what you hear, see, and find."

"I got chu, big bro. I know the hood like my backhand," he agreed with a big ole smile.

I know he was ecstatic to build with his older brother alone, so that offer didn't stay in the air more than a half-second.

Smokey cut his eyes over to his sisters, smirking. "VeeBee, and VeeBaby. Both of y'all are getting home schooled from now on. Everything a pretty girl can do in a classroom, she can do the exact thing even better at home on a computer. Chris will get to do something when he feels comfortable also. Mama, I just want you to quit working, and let me be that hard-headed ass son of yours please." He laughed, pointing a finger at me.

"Boy, you bumped yo head."

"Nah foreal, Ma, put in a two-week notice. I need you off the scene for a while." He straightened his expression to show the seriousness of his theory.

I shook my head, wondering what the hell he was about to get me into. He was moving so fast, I was gonna have to put a seatbelt across his head before he wrecked from over-thinking.

"Now, can anybody tell me where the hell we staying at? How's the area? What's the talk around the block?" He looked at all of us for answers.

O.J. popped a soda and took a seat at the table. I didn't have to say much because he broke it down to the science for his brother. He was up and down these streets all through the night, so I knew everything was just his daily playground in the area.

"We in Kirkwood."

"Kirkwood Community?" Smokey said, like it was so unfamiliar to him.

"Yeah, Kirkwood, they call it Lil Mexico though. All the young kids my age do. It seems like we all have the same thing in common around our section," OJ added on.

"And what's that?"

"Dreams of being the biggest money getter," he spilled taking another swig of the soda.

I saw myself slapping that shit out his hand, 'cause he sounded just like Smokey when he was around the age of ten. I didn't need another lost child, which is why I was glad his brother was home to take lead.

"At least it's truth in that dream somewhere. This is why I do it, so you don't have to. I guess you know if there's a lot of traffic up through here too, huh?" Smokey questioned him again.

"It is. All the older guys sell stuff in front of the store all day. It's the most traffic I've ever seen."

Smokey nodded and looked over to his friend Keith. "I guess this worked out perfect."

"What's perfect? You know I need to be filled in on every inch you step," I replied to his remark.

"It's easy, Ma." He paced slowly around the table speaking. "I have a mission this time around. It's a new area. It's new money, I'm a new face who came to take a fool's place. I want it all and coming in second is not accepted. This entire Kirkwood area, the apartments, backstreets, corners, and hustlers. I want them all under me. Either by choice, or with force. The hood would be my first place to take over, and the entire city would more than likely be next. I'm just gonna start off with lil Mexico as y'all say."

He was grinning like a kid plotting a trip to the candy store. That was a face I knew too well. One that was surely going to make competition come back for more than some hustling tips. I just hoped my baby could dodge the shade as it came.

Chris Green

Chapter 12

Only the early bird got the worm, so you know I was out extra early in order to get a feel for the community. I strolled down a couple of streets. Ran into a few people I actually knew and spotted out damn near every trap that was serving. It was petty hustling at its best. I was coming with a new wave. I was gonna feed the hood and watch them bring the money back to my palms. Me and Keith had a bigger mission.

We wanted perfection. Not to keep it, but to cook it. Not only that. We were about to preplan a map of different states that needed our assistance, to give Atlanta a chance to simmer down.

I breezed around the plaza area of Kirkwood and happened to stop at the gas station. A few thugs hung about hustling, but I could tell they weren't gonna be in my way at all, just from the way they dressed. Most of the gangstas hung low in Bixby Court during the day, but the goons, trappers, robbers and killers partied to sunrise. I knew a little about the east side from my days of riding with T. Even though, it might take a few adjustments, I was gonna break this neighborhood, until the birds chirped my damn name while the sun was rising.

I bought a few things out the drink section of the BP and stepped back outside. I paused after a few seconds of staring in thin air. My chin felt like it dropped to the fucking concrete. A live police station was sitting directly across from me, as if it was the nearest McDonalds, or CVS Pharmacy. Cruisers were about in the parking lot, and niggas was slanging dope directly in front of the store, like it didn't exist. Just when I thought about getting the hell on, I turned around, and met eyes with a nigga posted a few feet away from me. He was too close for comfort, but his energy seemed to be laid back. He looked me up and down, nodding.

"Wassup with ya, homie? Welcome home, my nigga." He saluted me like I knew him from the reunion last night or some.

"Uh, I don't recall who you are again. How do you know me?" I checked his ass.

"Who don't know you, lil bro? Smokey himself. You one of the only young hustlers an older nigga can respect. I know what you be 'bout."

"You can't know what I be 'bout, 'cause you don't know me," I corrected him quickly.

His face balled up like I disrespected him and judging from his posture, he acted like he wanted some problems.

"Damn, my guy, just don't front on me like I'm having paper trouble or some." He spread out a huge stack of crispy Ben Franks like a Chinese fan. "I just recognize real when I see it. This Kirkwood, lil homie. We were bred like this, so the money motive is the only reason I approached you, fool. I guess every money getter don't think alike." He turned to walk away, as if I was the negative energy. I damn near had to self-check myself, and make sure I wasn't coming sideways, and destroying the bond on the block before I had a chance to build it.

"Say, bro, don't take it cold, man. It's just I'm new out here, and I not trying to get mixed in and sent back to jail. I'm fresh out so I just wanted to pace myself, before I fell and tripped. I'm Smokey, what's ya name?" I shook his hand like a gentleman.

"I'm Po Boy, bro, raised on the east side, born on the north. I'ma loner out here, man. I don't rock with niggas, just like you don't. Sometimes this shit get boring, and a nigga just need some real ones around him to make shit a bit more player. Hell, that was the only reason I even decided to approach you," he admitted truthfully.

I had to respect where he was coming from on the street aspect, but trust was always a trait I happened to lack with every time. In my head, something told me to walk off on the nigga. Instead, I stamped my first piece of respect in the hood. I shook his hand.

"It's all good, no harm done, man. I'm only for the money. It seems like an easy felony, sitting right across the curb from the cops' personal stop and shop though," I threw out there to see if this fool was retarded.

His eyes were glued elsewhere, as I spoke. His next statement forced me to turn around.

"Are those yo people or some, Smokey?"

I faced the opposite way and spotted the black Ford F-150 damn near sitting on the curb.

The engine was roaring, and I couldn't see anything through the dark windows. Just as I thought about heading back into the store for a slight second, the windows came rolling down slowly. I guess Po Boy saw the barrels before me, because he was pulling his gun, and snatching me to get down. The minute my feet moved, gunshots erupted from the truck.

Pop! Pop! Pop! Pop! Pop! Poc! Poc!

Po Boy wasted no time shooting back, 'cause his shit was going off directly by my ear. In the mix of hearing a bullet scratch the concrete. I pulled out the small Ruger 9mm Keith's uncle gave me the night before, from my hip. I immediately hit the trigger, gunning back not caring who it hit in the process. I was trying to stay on my feet and keep up with Po Boy at the same time.

The truck was now speeding off, letting off the last fleeing shots in the air to end the pandemonium. I was running like hell behind the gas station, and whatever trail Po Boy led us through. We ended up on a street full of houses. The police sirens could still be heard clearly through the pathway and going back that way was damn sho out of the question. All I could do was keep my feet beating the pavement, until I got a good distance off.

"Any idea who the fuck that was, man?" I asked through my deep breaths, still pacing.

"Nope. It's never no telling when we posted out there. Probably Edgewood crew, Maybe Arkwright niggas. You can never be too careful," he answered as we sprinted swiftly through another set of bushes. We ended up coming out on a main street a few blocks down, and I didn't hesitate to catch my breath. This nigga was standing there like he was ready for an extra mile, or some shit. I knew from there, it was gonna be far from a dull day. I was shot at, running with a nigga that was probably about to be my codefendant, and hadn't been on the east side for a full twenty-four hours.

It was already trying to crumble, before I had the shit standing up correctly. Lil Mexico was fit for a name, but slight security adjustments needed to be made if I was gonna try and lock down anything. It was time to skip on to plan two, and if these chess moves worked effectively, we would have a business running in no time.

Dialing Keith's number, I listened to every ring drag slowly, until he picked up.

"Yeah, wassup Smoke?" his voice was sluggish as if he'd just gotten up.

"Had a small problem, need to kinda get away from it. You wouldn't happen to be driving, would you?" I was moving a hundred miles an hour.

"Where are you?" he asked me quickly.

"I'll be where you dropped me off last time. Pull up." I ended the call.

The thought of Po Boy saving my life continued to replay in my head, as we got near the street where my mama's house rested. It damn sure wasn't loyalty, like that just running around on the regular. I had to respect his gangsta, and the fact I could've just been dead a few minutes prior.

"I owe you one, man, I appreciate that back there," I thanked him once more.

"Never a problem on that end, Smokey. Like I said, I'm just another hustler around the way."

I saw the content in his eyes, but I kept fighting against myself for some reason. Regardless of my emotions, I refused to let a true solider slip past me without at least trying to recruit him our way.

"I'm saying, you think that hustle of yours can stand firm with team effort?"

"Something I've never had to second guess."

After that statement, the deal was sealed, and I had my new shooter.

Chris Green

Chapter 13

White Boy Keith

The next few months had been great with me and Smokey on the move. Our foundation was increasing with every step, and I was trying to be sure we didn't crash off any miscellaneous mistake. After switching a few things around his block, we eventually took over the surrounding streets, and the finishing touches trimmed themselves. Since then, we began taking the loads on the road. Tennessee, Mississippi, that wasn't even half. I started to figure out the key when we began pushing up north, Ohio, North and South Carolina. A few northern spots people had never mentioned to us before.

Today was Smokey's day to shine, and I had to be sure he understood the importance of this deal. I was on my last thirty days in the penitentiary for violating and leaving the state of Georgia. I was lucky the judge spared me with a ninety-day confinement. It only left me one way to communicate with him until I was released, the damn wall phone.

Dialing his number, I waited for the annoying machine voice to stop talking and accept the call.

"Keith, I was waiting for your call, you caught me right before I clocked in for work."

His statement only confirmed he was in Queens, New York, preparing to seal my uncle one of the best plugs in the Big Apple.

"Yeah, I'm just now waking up, bro. I know you got a big day ahead of ya. Good luck," I replied to let him know we was on the same accord.

"Cool. This spot up here is kinda nice, hopefully after this, I can catch a nice trip to the Bahamas or something. At least, Florida."

I laughed at his humor, but I could sense he was nervous as hell. Traveling with fifteen keys upstate would easily tweak you, especially if you're not able to conduct the business accordingly with the buyers.

"I could see a trip to Daytona in a few weeks or so. Let's try and focus on having a good time in New York. I'm sure Pachi will be happy. Give him my greetings."

"Pachi? I thought his name was—"

I slammed the phone on the receiver, before Smokey could say anything else. Laughing to myself, I headed back for my cell. A man stepped in my way. I hadn't been in the system no more than forty days, so a beef couldn't exist.

"I don't mean no harm, young blood. I just think I got some information you really need to hear. It might help save you, or your friend's life."

I truly didn't know what the hell he was speaking on, and I didn't want to speak too fast.

"What friend might that be, because I'm lost here?"

"Smokey. I think he's in danger." He grabbed my attention when I heard my guy's name.

I folded my arms, because now this stranger had me kind of nervous. Motioning for him to step in my cell, I pulled up the door and dropped the flap.

"What's going on and who the hell are you?" I cut to the chase immediately.

"I know your friend Smokey. He hasn't seen me in a while, but I know something that's about to be tragic to him and his family if we don't speak. My name is Bear Cat," he said with a straight face.

Chapter 14

Chan's Spa and Healing

Manhattan, New York

Smokey

Hanging up the phone with Keith, I pulled down onto a side street in Manhattan and I realized I had the wrong spot. We fucked around and reversed it, heading back towards Brooklyn. Once we found Fulton Street, the spa business I was looking for appeared before my eyes. Po Boy was assisting me with extra sight, in case anything looked flaky.

Plus, one of Keith's men, Felipe, was instructed to come along, requested personally by his uncle. He seemed kind of weird because he rapped most of the trip. The word from Keith was still solid. He was a natural killer. His dreads would hide all that nasty deception until it was time to use it. That's why I kept him closer than any other.

Parking the car, we hopped out, heading inside the establishment. The bell sounded off when we entered. A small and frail Chinese man stood at the counter. He was reading a newspaper, with an old woman cleaning behind him. I noticed security sitting in a small room, directly behind them. I still played things cool and walked over to him.

"Excuse me, sir. I'm looking for Pachi," I said just above a whisper.

"ChanChi, and you're late. I suppose his nephew won't be joining us this go around?" He looked at me, his slanted eyes filled with anger.

I didn't want to aggravate this foreigner ass nigga, so I kept a clean mind to lock the deal. I had come too far to slip and tripping wasn't in my blood.

"His nephew gives his greetings and assures business will be handled the same. And we do apologize for being… twenty-six minutes late," I said sternly while glancing at my watch."

He glared at me for a second too long, and I could sense he was making Po Boy and Felipe uneasy. He rose from the chair before I broke the silence.

"They have to step outside. You can follow me," he ordered, disappearing into the back. I nodded to them in approval, grabbing the bag of product.

The small woman shooed them out the front door, and I quickly slid to the back to catch up with Chan. I found him posted in a room, a few doors down. The tinted light made it seem more like a night lounge. A few women draped in robes moved about as if he wasn't posted in the middle of their working area.

"Come in." He nodded.

Closing our distance. I didn't hesitate to hand over the keys. In the end, I was only there for one reason.

"It's all there, you can test it if you like," I shot out there to ensure him good business.

"No need, I'm sure Blue is still trailing around the usual avenues these days. Your word is trusted, but there is something I need to clarify, for future references. Come with Keith or come alone. It's been that way, and if Blue respects good business, he'll understand."

"I'm sure that all will be addressed, for us to make this ride smooth as possible. You have my word."

He smiled, pushing a small tote from underneath his chair. "Satisfaction, is a must. All numbers are correct. I'm sure you will tell Blue, if he remains faithful with rotations, he can remain my supplier," Chan confirmed before I picked it up.

"Indeed, I will."

"Excuse me, but I'm not sure if Keith explained the rules of my business?" he asked me with a raised brow, throwing me off guard.

I was just about to leave, and now I was stuck wondering what the hell he meant by that dumb ass remark he made. "Nah, I'm not familiar, but I'm sure I can comprehend."

"My spa. You have to get massage before you leave. Pick you two or three pretty Asians to help you, and the next thirty minutes are free. I'm sure your friends wouldn't mind waiting a second, would they?" He moved towards the exit, snapping his fingers at a few women.

A few gorgeous ladies approached me and dropped their robes as if I was a king. I could tell English was not in their native tongue, but actions were. They began to feel and touch me, not giving a damn about me brushing them off.

"Uh… Chan, no disrespect, but I didn't come for that. I'll really take a pass if you don't mind."

"But I do. After you enjoy my workers, they will let me know you weren't wearing a wire, and you're free to go. If that's okay with you?" he shot back.

I shot him a funny grin for a second but dropped the bag on the floor. "Which one of y'all the cleanest?" I shook my head.

Chris Green

Chapter 15

Atlanta Police Department

Detective Murray F. Brown

It was only 8:30 in the morning, and I was on my third cup of Joe. For the past few weeks, I had been stationed at the Atlanta Police Precinct to assist with the recent calls they'd been receiving in the area. More shootings, the traffic for the drugs was rising daily, and now I had an overdose on my hands, with a homeless citizen around East Atlanta. Chief had been on a rampage about cracking down on the pipelines where any drug, firearm, or murder seemed to be sliding through the cracks of our duty officers.

My boss walked inside my office and paused my thoughts. He was looking frustrated, and any time he paced in a circle silently, he was pondering on whatever needed to be said.

"Sir, is there a problem?" I tried to break the ice and see what mission I was about to be placed on next.

"You're damn right there is. Pressure from the governor, and mayor is spilling on Zone Six Precinct, and I don't have any answer to give them, son. We're falling behind, and if we can't crack down on the city and get it stable, we could be looking at resigning, or facing charges with the same criminals," he fumed, with aggravation to me.

"Chief Williams, I know this may sounds harsh, sir, but we work our asses off to help this city. It'll never be the superhero safe zone you want every second on the hour, but some of these crooked ass law officials should be behind a few walls too. The unit has to work twice as hard, but you have to lead us on how to go about it, Cap," I replied, trying to spread a better vision at what needed to happen.

Clasping his hands tight, a grumble came from underneath his breath. "You're right. I need you to alert all shift officers. All areas must be patrolled, watched, and raided within the next sixty days. I want you on the east, the Kirkwood, and Edgewood zone."

"What exactly do you want me to do, sir?" I tried to get my objective clear, so there were no sinkholes.

"I want every drug dealer, murderer and thug from the neighborhood thrown under the jail, until we get a name. Find out who's calling the shots and make him wish he never had an illegal thought poof inside of his small ass incompetent brain," he ordered before storming out.

Grabbing my suit jacket, I headed for the squad car. Whatever was lacing the streets, of the Kirkwood community was about to be exterminated out. Cuffs, or a casket.

***

Slip Rock

Oakland City Junkyard

June 20, 1990, was a day I would never forget. I had been at the junkyard for the past few days collecting extra dues to keep shit flowing correctly. Selling pussy was always the market, but lately the drugs had been slowing up horribly, causing my trap to fall. I had been sitting on the same shit for the last two weeks and could barely sell an ounce of white girl out of the junkyard. The junkies had slowed, even the young thugs that came to purchase the weight from me. Shit was just lacking.

I was posted in the front room of the duplex, inhaling on some good marijuana, as my number-one bread winner, Misty combed through my good hair. I never thought I would ever see myself, having to come up with a second plan to stay ahead, but I was clearly seeing the phases occurring with my business, as the days flew by.

"Copsssss!" I heard one of my lookouts burst through the front door, yelling in a panic.

The word *cops* was good enough for me to drop everything and rush to that work.

"Bitch, get rid of them guns, go!" I pushed Misty towards the kitchen, as I ran for the opposite side of our spot. Grabbing all the drugs from underneath the sofa, I broke for the first bathroom. Wasting no time, I started to rip open and pour out the dope, while I flushed. From the other side of the walls, I could hear the police making their entrance. The loud yelling confirmed that for me, but once I heard the K-9 Unit dog barking, my chest nearly fell out. I was moving quick as I could to get rid of the fed case sitting on the floor in front of me, but time just wasn't on my side.

The bathroom door crashing in forced me to jump up. I felt a hard right elbow connect with my chest, immediately putting me back down.

"Freeze, or ya head comes off next, motherfucker!"

He was holding the gun so close to my face, I could damn near see the bullet. I wanted to buck so bad, just from the extra aggressive shit he was pulling, but I knew there was no such thing as a win, when it came down to fucking with the pigs.

"It's kinda clear I'm down, fuck man, what the fuck you using all the extra force for, honkey?"

He threw me in cuffs, lifted me from the ground, and smiled. "Because I'm just a honkey that don't like monkeys. Now, keep your mouth shut before I break your jaw next."

As he led me out the front door of my spot, my eyes landed on all the surrounding cars. Nearly the entire block was out, and it wasn't even near afternoon time. I knew then, somebody was talking. I was the only successful business on the southwest, maintained that for years without making shit hot, and I watched it all fall within a day. I knew my conclusion was positive when my eyes met Detective Murray Brown walking over to me with a devilish grin.

"Mr. Carter, or should I say, Slip Rock himself? It's been a while since I seen you shining with them million-dollar bracelets on ya wrist. Tell me, how does it feel?" He held a hand in front of my mouth like a microphone.

"You know, it's a real great feeling, like when your wife used to spit on it." I grinned, knowing that shit would rattle his skin. It felt good to fuck a cop's wife, especially when he knew your name specifically from crawling in her guts.

Punching me in the stomach with his right fist, I heaved over, coughing violently. He kneeled down beside me, with a hand on my shoulder. "You have a death wish, punk. My wife had to be weak and pathetic to screw a worthless 1970s pimp, that's addicted to slanging smack. You're nothing! But guess what I'm gonna do for ya? You'll help me find out where the drugs are falling in the city, and I'll make sure you don't spend the next fifty years in solitary confinement."

"You might as well pull your gun and shoot me in the head, Brown, 'cause our conversation has finally ended."

He forced a laugh, motioning his officer to take me away. His last few words tumbled through my head, before I was escorted away.

"I'll take you, family, friends, or whatever is necessary off the streets until it ends, Carter. I won't stop until it ends."

Chris Green

Chapter 16

White Boy Keith

After finishing up my last few weeks in the feds, I was back on the streets with Smokey, running headfirst. Of course, we had the sales rising again, now I was able to show my face for the connections to be at ease.

Smokey had been applying himself well, and eventually moved up in good graces with Uncle Blue. The more he'd seen we could handle on our own, the more he started to open up different avenues for us to cross. The normal fifteen was starting to boost up to thirty, and the quicker we sold the product, the faster we could stack the cash. It all came hand in hand.

It was small shit that fell our way, like the incident of me running into the guy Bear Cat in prison. He was feeding me stories about Smokey's dad having some bad blood lingering around, and for some reason, he felt it was going to haunt Smokey and the family if they weren't aware. Me telling my arrogant friend that, only encouraged him to hire more watchers, workers, and push the product even harder. I could see him molding into a true hustler with his skills, and he was refusing to show any weakness. It was just the way we had to be. Now that we were running smooth as oil, my uncle finally gave the call I'd been waiting for.

While I was bagging up the money from our last transaction, my phone started to vibrate, and I picked it up quickly.

"Yeah?"

"Keith, I have good news. Things have been great, nephew. You gotta tell me one day how you became so smart," he spoke with excitement.

I could hear women laughing in the background, and judging from his slurring voice, he had been drinking. I knew whenever he celebrated, it meant something great was ahead.

"I guess it runs in the blood, old man. You know I love good news," I replied, stepping a distance away from Smokey, Po Boy, and Felipe.

"You've done well with keeping us in the game. It's a mutual respect between businessmen to do more good business after that foundation has been laid. You have a trip to take in the next few days. Florida. When you lay your understanding with this man, you'll never have to worry about a dry day again in the state of Georgia. This is your time to shine, nephew. I need to know, can you handle this?" he questioned me.

That was an understatement when it came to me doing what I did best. I was always on point with the objective at hand, but I still evaluated all points to make sure I knew what was at hand.

"So, what are we looking at this time?" I asked.

"Fifty."

Hearing the number, I turned to add the total up in my mind. Before I could estimate it, my uncle answered, as if he was reading my mind.

"Nine hundred thousand."

"Okayyyy." I scratched my head, knowing I've never dealt with so much beforehand.

That was damn near a million-dollar ticket, and the thought of getting fifty kilos back from Florida to Georgia was gonna take some serious brain storming.

"Whew, I've never handled anything like that," I replied truthfully.

"I know, but this will also mold you from this day on. We rise to gain, and eventually you have to move on to bigger things. Enjoy yourself while you're down there. Sometimes you need joy in this middle-minded life we have, just not too much, so the business savvy will stand strong and confident, even if it was the first time you've handled twenty bucks. I have faith in you as always."

"I'm sure you do." I ended the call and moved back over the working table.

I was forming the new mission in my mind, when I caught Po Boy eyeing me on the low. Since we'd met, I've had a dislike for the strange dude. On the strength of Smokey, I held my peace. We were so busy with making sure all the pieces fell in line, anything else was obsolete.

"We got another trip on our hands, and I mean a big one. We might have to take a vacation in the process."

Smokey caught my remark, looked over at me. "Sounds like a plan, where we headed?

"Disney World." I shrugged my shoulders.

Chapter 17

Disney World, Orlando, Florida

Po-Boy

It had been an amazing trip since we had arrived in the Orlando, and I had to admit, it was gonna be more than a pleasure to let my mama see this payday, and major payback that was long overdue. A day my father didn't uphold. Miami T was the reason, so his son Smokey fell into the damn pit, for being fucking related. It was just gonna have to be a bad day for the fellas, and I was literally walking less than a hundred steps of this bread.

The elevator alerted us that we had reached the fifteenth floor. The doors opened, leading to a two-way hall. One says, East, another West. Smokey was looking confused, but humble as always, and White Boy Keith, hunched over with one hand gripping a bad, Cuban-looking chick's breast. She had to be a model. I still didn't give a fuck., they were getting robbed. One security rode in with us, and I know he didn't play with handling the business. Coolio. If my uncle's shottas was on point, we were about to get paid.

"Where the hell do we put this?" Keith laughed, sliding the key card repeatedly across the pad.

The brown marble oak doors popped open, allowing us entrance to a sighting you only catch in one of them rich-ass movies with them upper elite muthafuckas. I knew these niggas either were police or working with some Columbians sho nuff. I pressed the call button on my cell phone to let my crew activate.

"Damn, this shit is beautiful." Smokey walked over to the massive window, sitting down a duffle bag.

Keith's little daughter sprung happily towards the first room, which gave me the perfect opportunity. I pulled out my gun so quickly, they all had to laugh and double take to be sure they weren't seeing the demon rise in me.

"No screaming. No talking, no flinching, or I'm killing every last one of y'all. Go ahead and test me out." I aimed my strap, pulling another one from my back, aiming at Coolio.

Keith's wife, Jasmine, immediately started to tremble when she witnessed my four back-up hitmen slide through the front entrance like invited guests. Two of them wore black suits, with guns by their side. The other two wore plain causal gear, with the "surfer lame of the year award" appearance. But straight silent murderers that walked light stomped heavy. The room grew quiet, and Keith looked back and forth between me and Smokey. He pulled his wife close and spoke humbly.

"What do you want, and why are you doing this?" His facial expression was cold, but weak at the same time. I immediately took control.

"You can thank your friend Smokey for the money you had for the plug down there on twelfth floor. Room 1203. Yeah, we had to scoop that lil bread and to be honest, I wouldn't have known about any dope unless you guys spoke about it. Hear my drift." I smirked at Keith wickedly.

"Fuck ass snake. I knew you been looking greasy all the way down here, and now you wanna pull this?" he snarled, swelling up like a giant bear. His moves were very tempting, but I didn't budge, neither did his big ass when I raised my suppressed Glock 40 handgun.

"I told you earlier before this, baby boy. This shit was for the white guy. You had to keep saving ol captain ass nigga, huh?"

You're dead," he replied calmly with clenched hands.

Smirking, I looked back at my killers. "Search 'em all. Take everything valuable. Find the dope, and if they move or buck, shoot they ass on the spot."

A cellphone started to ring, and all silence fell again. I could tell it was Smokey's from how he was flinching his scary ass pupils up and down, nervous as shit.

Walking over to him, I pulled it from his pocket, and answered without looking. "I'm sorry. He's being robbed at the moment. dial back after regular hours." I laughed into the receiver before tossing it across the room.

The sight of Keith's daughter coming back out of the room, caused one of the shooters to flinch and fire his gun without remorse.

BOOM!

I felt Smokey reach for my arm and the tussling began. We nearly fell over the glass coffee table, until I leveled the gun at his forehead, forcing him to calm down.

"Don't make me kill you, fat boy. Now where the fuck the work!" I was slobbering in rage like a zombie, craving for flesh. They could tell from my bulging eyeballs, I probably would kill a person within the next few moments, and they panted for help.

"Keith, give it to him," Jasmine mumbled in tears as he searched his child for a gunshot wound.

The other guys with me were bearing down with force, holding their guns and intensifying the risk, if they continued to move stupid. Keith stumbled when he noticed the gunshot landed in his lower leg. His vision raised to mine, burning with the quote *why* deep in his eyes.

"It's not here, this isn't the room where I ordered the work to drop. You got the money. just leave!"

His hands were balled in anger, but I cared nothing about his emotions, it was especially 'bout mines, and the reason we traveled all the way from mean ole Bama town. This shit was personal.

"Well, I guess you better get to popping them chops on where it's at!" I spat.

Smokey's phone began to ring again, an that's when the call from my other men, buzzed on the radio. "We have to leave. The cops have been alerted!" a voice shot through my earpiece.

There were only four men on the other side, and risking them was gonna be difficult holding nine hundred grand. The eight keys of good kept weighing in my mind when I finally took a deep breath. I quickly watched my men search the suite with ease. My eyes drifted downcast to my watch every ten seconds, as they moved around.

"We gotta go, grab whatever we got and let's go. Let's go now," I ordered, still with my gun still pointed stiffly at Smokey's head.

Grabbing the duffle from the floor, I backed away to the door. "I guess our time is up for now, but it won't be if I see y'all face before we get to where we heading. Do yourself a favor. Wait in the room for an hour before you get help. Enjoy the rest of your time at Disney World." I smiled, falling out of the room.

My guards eased out behind me, and ensured the elevator arrived before taking the stairs down to the exit parking deck. My cell vibrated, alerting that I had a call.

"Yeah?" I placed my ear up to the receiver.

"He fucking got away."

Chapter 18

Miami T

Vee's Home, 9:33 pm

It was a little after nine when the cab driver pulled up to Vee's driveway. I could see the lights on, and a few shadows moving around inside from the silhouettes on the curtains. I scanned the area before stepping out,

"Listen. I only need ten minutes and I'll be back, keep the car running."

The Arab shook his head at me but acted as if he understood my words clearly.

Standing straight, I headed for the door, and quickly rang the bell when I reached the porch. I could see a few cars moving up, and down the main road but I paid it no attention. My mind was only on one thing, getting my family the fuck out of Georgia.

Hearing the locks opening startled me for a second, but I quickly smiled and moved inside when Vee's face popped on the opposite side. Pushing her inside, I closed the door, locking lips with my baby mama like we never had before.

"Boyyyy, why didn't you tell me it was today." She started to giggle and hug me tightly.

"Listen, baby, I gotta tell you something, and we gotta talk about it as we get the kids, and y'all away from here."

Linda, my oldest son Chris and my girls came out of the living room, catching the moment, and all the love in the world seemed to float towards me. Linda was grabbing her a handful, with a mouth full of kisses, while my kids asked me every question they had been harboring for the past four years. I literally had to slow everyone down and grab Linda's hands.

"Look, I missed you guys a lot too, but I need y'all to hear me out for a second. Go upstairs, pack all the kids' important info. I gotta get you and Vee out of here. It's hard to explain, but we might be in danger if we stay here."

"T, what the hell are you talking about? You just got here. It's almost ten at night. I keep calling your son, and can't get no answer. He gone be happy to know you're finally back home." Vee waved me off.

"Linda, do what I said, please." I pointed my finger towards the stairs.

Once I watched her gather our seeds, taking them to the upper floor, I gazed over to Vee with a calm, but serious face. "Baby, I know this ain't what you wanna go through within my first hours out, but I know something is wrong. I need you to head down to Cabbage Town, and duck off at a friend of mines house named Stacy. She will protect y'all like family, until I can come pick you guys back up. Me and Smokey might have to handle a few things to make sure no problems follow us at all. I can't lose y'all anymore, Vee." I gazed down at her with pure empathy floating through my veins.

"And how long will this last? Huh, T? Until you catch another bid, or get my baby boy killed?"

By the time her words escaped her mouth, Linda was coming back down the steps, with all the kids marching right behind. They all stood behind her, waiting for my next words, me finally being the man of my house again. I kissed them all one by one and grabbed Vee's hands. "Trust me and know that we're gonna be okay. please." I rubbed the back of her hand gently

The sound of screeching tires forced me to look out of the front blinds hastily. I spotted two cars blocking off the cab and immediately, three men jumped out of one car with assault rifles, checking the inside. I could hear the old Arab scream for help, and I sprang straight into action.

Running back over to Vee and Linda, I pushed them and the kids to the back door. "Go now! Vee, you keep everyone together, and don't move until you hear from me!"

Linda rushed out the back door, heading the opposite way, with the kids jogging behind. Vee walked over to the kitchen counter, snatching the 9mm pistol from the second shelf. Cocking it back. she put it in my hands, following up with a kiss. "Don't die if you don't have to. Come back and get us, or I'll never wait again." She rushed out the door to catch up with Linda.

Cutting off the kitchen light, I moved smoothly through the hallway, hitting every switch I passed. The house was now pitch black, and I was hunched over in the corner, peeking from the window as four armed men, walked in my yard. I couldn't tell a face, but truly it didn't even matter.

Stepping into the dining room hallway, I leveled my gun for the door, waiting. My skin crawled with adrenaline, and before I could blink again, my front door was crashing in. I wasted no time firing up every face I saw. The first slug struck the one entering, forcing him straight to the floorboard.

Boom! Boom! Boom! Boom!

"Y'all want war, motherfucker! Let's play then!" I snapped, letting off four more shots.

The thought of my kids and women made me grow rage inside my heart. One way or the other, every nigga holding a gun towards me at that moment was officially about to die.

Chapter 19

Smokey

It was hectic after the police arrived at the scene of the crime. Keith had to be rushed to a hospital. I was being questioned by three different detectives, trying to place the entire scenario down in one conversation. I kept quiet, allowing Keith's wife to be the mouth for us all. According to her story, a masked man tried to rob us after we arrived to the fifteenth floor, and that's what we were all going by, if we wanted to make it out of the hotel back up to Atlanta.

The safety of Rhestay's money was at bay, and we were now at odds with the same man, flooding the happy state of Georgia. I was standing next to a cruiser with Keith's daughter, when his wife was escorted back over to us.

"We've been cleared to go, guys. Let me sign a few papers for Keith to transfer to Atlanta, and we can head on to the hospital, until they fixed him up properly." She shook her head at me with a look of relief.

I wasn't. My mind was tracing around a tracking field like a runner, sprinting on their final lap. I was devastated and wanted blood on my hands to sooth that torment. The entire way to the hospital, I remained quiet. Once we arrived, I headed in with Coolio, and Keith's wife beside me. When we entered the room, his eyes landed on me, and waved a hand. "Y'all give me a minute with Smokey to discuss something." he asked, calmly. Displeasure was written on his expression.

Instead of replying, Coolio, his wife and child turned to exit the room, closing the door behind them. All I could hear for a slight second was the beeping on different medical machines. I moved towards Keith, taking a seat next to the bed.

"How does this happen to good people, Smokey? I mean, where the hell did this come from?" He gazed over at me.

I exhaled a with no clean answer. "Truthfully, Keith, I blame all this shit on me. If I wouldn't have brought bitch man around. no robbery could've taken place. I let a wolf in our circle, and he crept in with another pack. I don't care how it may look, my nigga. I won't sleep until buddy die for his treason. I can put my life on that." I patted my chest hard, while looking at him seriously.

"My daughter could've been killed, My wife. We lost nine hundred grand, and we are turning over into a beef that's about to be over our heads. I want you to find that motherfucker. Kill him and hang his ass from the street pole downtown. Get back everything. Send however many we have to. No matter what it cost. Tell me you can get rid of this dude?" Keith folded his arms with hostility in his posture.

Everything he was spitting was true shit, and the more he spoke, I felt like a true lame. It was never a day where I would get my own shit taken by a nigga. But having a man who respected me in juvie ends up helping me run up a hundred grand, crib, and new whip since me touching ground was something nobody's ass could just blast about.

It showed me then that money didn't mean shit, the dope was only sold to get the profit, which still meant business, but not really shit. It was our blood that was sacred. That's when you know there's love, when a nigga takes your soul as serious as if it was his own. He was literally the closest person to me on the streets at that moment.

Instead of playing it miserable, I used that for my fuel, and tightened up.

"I can and I will, bro. You're my friend before this money, so this shit is personal. Just get back to Atlanta and worry about the rest. I'm about to go, make this happen." I stood to my feet, heading for the door.

Before I walked out, I looked back. "Nobody touches any of us and walks away, bro. Period," I stated, pacing out into the hall.

I nodded at his wife and Coolio, continuing for the main entrance. Getting back to our rentals, I jumped in the front seat of the truck, cranking the engine. My cellphone forced me to dig in my pocket, to answer the incoming call.

"Yeah, what is it?" I mumbled, backing out the parking space.

"Smokey, I've been blowing your phone up, baby boy, we need you. Please!" I heard my mama stress with grief.

"Mama, what's wrong? What happened, slow down and talk to me."

"Your father's home, but I don't know if he's still alive. We have some people looking for us, and a few stopped by my house. He was there but didn't leave with us. I'm scared and confused."

"Just calm down, I'm on the way. Who's doing this to y'all?"

"Your father wanted me to tell you to watch out for Po Boy. Please get back to us."

I shuddered, hearing the con artist's name and grew furious. "Text me the address where you at. I'll be there soon. Don't move." I hung up the line, mashing the gas out of the parking lot.

Heading for the expressway, I jumped on, doing the dash back to Atlanta with one mission. Kill Po Boy, and everyone that stepped across the state line with him.

Chapter 20

Smokey

After the incident with Keith down in Orlando, I got the call from my mama, about things not looking right, and immediately headed back from Atlanta. It took me nearly seven hours to make it to my destination, but I pushed the pedal to the floor to make there in a timely fashion.

Pulling on the westside, up to the abandoned Anderson Park Elementary School. It was beyond ducked off, and surely a place to handle a serious issue if you happened to need some privacy.

Stepping out of my truck, I made my way to the side of the building. Pulling out my strap, I made my way through a creaky, medal door. Silence illuminated the walls inside, and I was prepared to handle any bullshit that decided to present itself.

Strolling down the narrow hallway, I found the second-grade school corridor. Heading to the third room on the left-hand side, I paused before entering.

Felipe was in movement, with a pair of black gloves over his hands. A thin razor was between his fingers, slicing through the skin of Po Boy's cheekbone.

His breathing was erratic and from the size of his swollen face, and busted eye, I could tell he was suffering through whatever had taken place before I arrived. I smirked with comfort. Exhaling my relief that this fuck nigga would meet his fate after I spoke my piece.

"Wassup, big man? I thought I would keep him breathing until you made your presence known. I know you may want the honors personally," he offered with a wicked smoke, holding the hand knife out to me.

I declined with a head shake and kneeled down in front of Po Boy's bitch ass. Blood drooled from his nose and lips like a faucet, causing bubbles to form at the tip of his lips. I knew he was past done, and it wasn't much to prove and know but his death and whoever the fuck played a part in having me, and Keith set up. Coolio? Janet? Rhestay? I didn't know what the fuck to think, but I wasn't leaving until I found out something.

"Aye, nigga, wake the fuck up." I snapped my fingers a few times, before slapping him across the face.

His body shifted to look up at me, and I spotted the fear rolling down that nigga stomach as if he had to take a shit. He began to mumble incoherently, but I quickly shushed him with my finger.

"I trusted you, and it fell back against me like everybody else knew it would. Being too friendly was never in my vision for hustling or earning the loyal friends I had beside me. I just moved accordingly, pacing along without any stumbles."

"It wasn't for you, Smokey. You just couldn't stay out of the way of helping this white boy. He's a lick nigga!" he struggled to speak, as I posted in front of him.

"Nah, you got it twisted, idiot. That's my brother, a man whose shoes you could never fill. You made the action, but you didn't play out the scene coming behind it. You touched the wrong person, and that's something I can't let go unanswered. I'll give you a second to think about what you need to say to me. I wanna know who, and why?"

He started to move around in the seat, shifting his weight to one side before smiling.

"I'm already lost, Smokey. You can't hurt me anymore than I hurt myself, nigga. This is only the beginning to our catastrophe, and we won't rest until Miami T's head is resting over our family's mantelpiece. You can stamp that shit." He swallowed hard, before spitting to the side of his chair.

I folded my arms, recognizing just how slimy and fucked up dude was. He had no morals or principles and having mercy upon him was something I couldn't see escaping from my heart. It was no more asking, no negotiations.

Staring him in the eyes, I slid the Desert Eagle from my side, placing one into the chamber. I didn't show any form of remorse, or even give him the slightest indication I was letting him get to me.

"You see, Po Boy, that's where the fuckery comes in at. I've never been good with copping pleas, and quite frankly, I have no intentions on starting. You never mattered, and I'm glad this small stumble was able to expose your true colors. Unfortunately, you won't be able to pull the trickery on anyone else, thanks to your fuck-up. It's appreciated from all the hustlers throughout the city."

"Fuck you, pussy. Nothing can stop your death. Not even God, Smokey."

I tilted my head looking down at the retard talk recklessly. He didn't even know my mind was already made up with the decision on what was to come next, and before he could keep running his gums. I aimed the Desert Eagle at his forehead and pulled the trigger.

Boom!

The blood from his head splattered across my hands, and shoes, after catching the first slug through his jaw.

His screams were now fading into mumbles, as I aimed for a second time. Once the bullet escaped my gun, it found home in the center of Po Boy's head, killing him instantly.

I watched his tied-up body drop to the floor from the force of my gun and took a deep breath. The incident with the clown was placed to rest, but I knew more was surely about to come about for the death of this nigga whenever they located his body. The next steps were simple. Take out everything that played a position with Po Boy, and make sure it never occurred again. Even though I was furious about my current situation, I had to maintain in order to make sure I made it out alive.

"Felipe, I want everybody to know how we stepping after this day. No more friends. No more employees. All business is dealt strictly through me or Keith. At least, until everybody dies that had anything to do with this. Clean this place up, and when the time is right, dump his ass somewhere nice," I ordered before tucking the pistol back on my waist to leave.

"Sure thing, big bro, just let me know who got to die before you go." He chuckled before loosening the restraints on the lifeless body

"Just stay low for a few days. I'm gonna slide around, checking a few temperatures to see if I can put this to an end. If I can't, then I'll go at it until we can't push on with it anymore."

"Done like today, Smokey." He saluted me before I made my exit.

Making it back to the front of the school, I headed back for my truck, and felt the vibration of my phone. Forced me to dig it out my pocket, before jumping into the driver's seat.

"I'm on my way, I'll be there in ten minutes," I spoke through the line, quickly ending the call.

I didn't need to have any conversations at that moment, besides my foot meeting my gas pedal to reach my next spot. I had to get down to the bottom of a mystery that had me speechless. At that moment, it didn't matter what else I found out, whoever was a part of the mishap was gonna suffer just as the rest. That was my word to the code of the streets.

Chapter 21

Miami T

Cabbagetown

Since I had gotten home, Vee and I only had so much that we had to catch caught up on due to my recent run-ins with the past. It still didn't make me forget to admire that I cuffed a beautiful, and loyal baby mother to stand beside me, as I trailed through my journeys. I never knew we would end up with the lifestyle we currently lived, but I wasn't complaining, neither was I willing to trade it in.

The sound of a car pulling into the parking lot of Stacy's apartments forced me to stiffen my posture, just in case I had to handle the business on any more unwanted guests from out of state. The sound of a car door opening caused Tracy to walk towards the door, pistol in hand. She was crooking her neck to side like an owl, glaring out of the peephole quietly. After a few seconds, she turned to look at me and Vee before opening the door.

I watched my son step inside the threshold, looking like a fresh printed image of me when I was in my early twenties. He had grown for his age, and I was proud to say my young thug had held it down since I fell victim to the incarceration system. His mug was firm and right as we met eyes, he moved directly towards me. My instincts told me to stand up, not sure on how he would respond to the recent bullshit now railroading us.

"Look, son, I know you're mad, but rest your temper and try to think of a resolution, instead of going at my neck." I held up my hands, not wanting to have an altercation.

After being away from them so long, all I truly wanted was for their happiness to overweigh the clouds of calamity. Somewhere down the line, I ruptured that mission even more.

"I wanna know why the fuck your name coming up inside of my business going sour, because those actions almost got a friend of mine and his family killed. Hatred is wrapped around your name like a wedding band, Pop. It runs through the city like a runaway train, and after all the years of me finally making my way, you come to tear it back down." His words dragged out as if I was his biggest enemy in the field.

I had to give a frown that he knew all too well, from the low blow comment. I held my composure, still knowing my son had a right to be entitled to his low, but true statement. It was all in the process of regrowing and deleting these annoying ass people for good. Instead of holding back any longer, I told them the truth.

"About eleven years back. I ran into some trouble down in Alabama with some friends of mine. We made a move for some money, and my friend ended up being murdered, by me. I know his brother and nephews are more than likely behind this."

"What's this guy's issue, and it is a secret way to squash this, or could somebody please alert me on what we got going on here?"

All I could see was Vee's face balled up harder than a fist, and before I knew it, she was trying to bomb in my shit.

"You dirty motherfucker, you mean to tell me this is about that hoe Tracey? Fresno too, huh? I guess that's why I see Cheno all down here creeping like he got a chip on the shoulder?" she asked me with her nose stuck up in the air.

"Not wholly, but yes, Vee."

Her hand batted me across the face with the quickness, but I did my best to try and dodge it. Her finger was aimed for me sturdily, with looks of death blazing through her flesh.

"You mean to tell me this is all about this bitch, T? You got my son and family out here on edge for your nasty cheating habits with a married woman. My heart still goes out to Fresno and his family."

Her arms folded angrily, and from the look on my boy's face, I was in the blender for not being able to control my flamboyant lifestyle and controlling desires. It blinded me in the past but crippled my future even harder.

"Vee, Smokey, I know the both of you are pretty upset with a few bad decisions I made. Hell, it's had me paranoid to this day, but everything I confined myself into out there on that turf was for us, even if it was to get in a better position for y'all to live better."

"What about asking how we feel on that matter? Emotions run more than one way, T. You've been this boastful, big-timer since you were a teenager, and it's done nothing but cause us pain and more drama. We could've quit. Just lived normally like all the other normal couples floating around this world," she huffed with exhaustion.

My son went to her side, rubbing a hand across her shoulder. "Be easy, Ma. I'm gonna handle this. One way or the other, but I need his help to do it." He cut his eyes over to me, secretly daring me to keep causing the dreadful pain on his mother's mental. Of course, I took my lick on the chin like a man and accepted my son's invitation to have my family back at my side.

"I'll do whatever need be, to get my shit in order for us. I just want it to end." I nodded in accordance.

"Well, I'm gonna be the first to tell you, I don't play about mines, but neither do I play about my dad, or close ones. I need to know everyone you know, and we need an estimated time to flush these snakes out of my video, or none of us might not be around to speak about it."

"I'm down for what you're saying, Smokey, but we can't just push on these people as if they are nobodies. We need a real plan," I voiced to him, just for a warning.

He stood quietly between me, and his mother for a few seconds before replying.

"I think I got that under control. I just need you to follow my lead and stay put until I give the green light," he said, heading for the door.

***

Smokey

Blue's House

Sliding into the parking lot of Blue's home, I spotted Keith stepping out of his truck, being escorted by Coolio. I hopped out of my whip and pushed up to his side. The crutches he was walking on, shook slightly as we moved for the front door. I noticed a few other cars, aligned in the driveway, so I was guessing Blue was in the mix of handling business.

"Are you okay, bro?" I held on to one of his shoulders.

"Sss, yeah, I don't think I have a choice. Besides a bullet in my leg and being robbed by a fucking flunky, I'm A-okay."

I shook my head at his statement, but I couldn't fault him for feeling salty for the snake ass move resting on my face card.

I was about to reply to his remark as we entered the home, but the group of men posted on the opposite side of

Blue's couch, forced me to pause. I wanted to reach for my gun but held my composure in case we were pulling into an ambush.

"What the hell is going on?" Keith asked, looking around at the dread head Bahamians, mugging like death was the only thing we had to speak on.

"Keith, as always, it is an honor to see you again. It's the young hustler himself, eh? Me and your uncle Blue here were just speaking about our little mishap of this money and transaction. So, I made my way across the water, just to see you fellas face-to-face."

"Listen, Rhestay, I've always handled things accordingly when it came to our ties in this business. I slipped and got took off. I got numerous men out, finding out who made the approach to even put their life at risk. I'm literally lost for words on how this shit happened." He cut his vision over to me, silently showing me that shit was probably about to get ugly if these dudes made the wrong move inside of his home.

"Ayee, mon, I just asked a question, my friend. I mean, nine hundred thousand dollars isn't the average check you witness drop back into a man's pocket when it has been taken. That leaves me in the blind when I'm searching for the answers that truly means the most. So, do tell me, Keith, how do you expect to get my money back?"

Before he could even open his mouth, I stepped forward, taking control over the entire conversation.

"I don't mean any disrespect, Rhestay, but I stand firmly on what I do. I played a position in parts of this fumbling and part of me can't allow Keith to take the blame himself. I am willing to do whatever in order to catch these bitches and deliver their heads and money back to your feet. I also know everyone is liable for a slip-up. I'm only asking for your patience to allow us, in fact, even make sure you are reimbursed fully. I mean, we've hustled this far."

The powerful man smirked, leaning back against the couch as if he were lost for words, but part of me felt he respected where my mind was just lingering at.

"You seem like a true friend, big mon. One that is willing to win, or even lose for this friend. I respect that strong ambition, it births loyalty. Something most can't acquire. I sell my drugs to Blue because we have done great business in the past, present, and of course for the near future. but we have rules that must be followed, son."

"And were the right ones to carry those orders out, that's a promise I'm guaranteeing, fuck worrying about how Keith feels," I added, trying to keep him far away out of the picture.

Blue remained on the couch quiet with his legs crossed as if it was all just a normal day, but I could see he was clearly aggravated from the words being exchanged. As Rhestay stood to leave, his men moved like his feet and arms, with every step he took.

"Maybe we can link in a few days or so for a count up of... say, about two hundred thousand. That should be sufficient enough to keep the animosity on the floor for at least a month or so. I'll be in you guys' city for about six weeks. That should be more than enough time to have our debt cleared away to do more business." He waved a hand to one of his men.

The foreign man carried a huge black duffle, dropped it aggressively on the floor, and continued to move behind his boss.

"That's a gift to you boys from me, eh? Sixty kilos. You keep eight from each block and turn in the rest. Just a little work consignment while I wait for my money to be gathered. Maybe next time we can meet on better terms, Blue,"

Rhestay added, stepping out of the bounds of my uncle's home.

We moved with him until he reached the door, replying back to the indirect threat.

"Rhestay, I respect you as a friend and as a businessman, but the next time you approach my humble casa, I would like you to self-check your attitude and posture, or just go ahead and murder me once our eyes meet. I'm sure you can accept those wishes as you depart from our grounds," Blue checked.

"Respect, warrior," he shot back, before getting in the tinted vehicles to exit the premises.

I couldn't help but to face the two men I went into business with, after the recent encounter with their plug. It wasn't sitting right, and it was gonna be my job to show that we could fix it.

"Listen, fellas, I know it might seem shaky right now, but don't lose faith in me. We're gonna smooth this shit out, but it's a process. I still need to know I have you boys' blessing to move around to establish that," I explained, hoping their minds could feel my reasoning.

"Things are smooth with or without you helping, Smokey. The problem is literally Rhestay. He's a man of ambition when it comes to the game, and if he finds a way to rise above competition, he'll take that chance by any means necessary. We have to double hustle and beat him to the beat. Pay him off. Get rid of any people that seems to share hatred for you both and repay me in the next life for saving ours tonight."

"How do you suppose we double hustle, and be in the mix of a hot ass homicide at the same time?"

Easy, the same way you hustled, and allowed them to take it, the same way you can step it up and earn it back quicker." Blue nodded at Keith, and swiftly departed up the giant staircase to the second floor.

"So, where do we go from here?" I asked him, not trying to put a rush on us by moving too quickly.

He thought a second before answering. "I have a spot out on Donnelly that can assist us with a few things. We might have to tweak a few adjustments to make it all perfect, but it's our only opportunity to get what we need too, in a timely fashion." He stood up on the crutches, heading for the door.

Instead of asking questions, I just followed behind, preparing myself for whatever needed to be done. At the end, it was us against them all. Regardless of what falls. We were gonna shut the streets down with our names, and still reign on top. That was my fucking promise.

***

P&J's Trap

Donnelly Street

Keith

After getting to our destination on the southwest, I turned into the home and shut off my engine. The night sky was just starting to fade across the heavens, and all I could remember was the nerve of this nigga Po Boy, knocking me down for everything I worked hard to reach. It made me stronger inside, but it also made my heart crumble with all the trust issues. Money was gonna be the new top priority, and when that obligation seemed to be violated, I would take the next precautions on making sure my empire never stumbled again.

Smokey and I stepped out my car, heading around to the back porch. It was extra dark from the tall trees overhead, but we still managed to make it up the staircase without tripping over a dead body.

Once I reached the top step to tap the burglar bar, the sound of an assault rifle racking back, rattled through my ears.

Smokey reached for his pistol, when we noticed the man on the roof aiming down at us recklessly.

"Who dat? If you two on the jack move. Y'all fools better high step it the fuck back up outta here," a voice boomed angrily.

Once I realized who it was, I shook my head, making Smokey ease his tension.

"Yeah, and if you don't wanna be out of a job and a place to stay, you'll get off the top of the damn house, and let me in please." I leaned my head to the side impatiently.

"Oh, shit. Is that you, Keith?" G-man asked before jumping down from the short roof onto a rundown deep freezer.

"Nah, it's the Quiznos sub guy from downtown that split my sack with you last week. Of course, it's me, jackass."

He moved with the quickness, rushing over to us. His grill was browner than the usual smile, but he greeted me, with the same enthusiasm as he did when we encountered each other on the usual.

"My fault, Keith. You know I can go over top sometimes, but Janet and Pauline won't have it any other way," he addressed, while double tapping the back door twice in a rhythm.

It wasn't a few seconds before the slide passed the locks unrestrained and opened up. Pauline stuck her head out, gazing at us all before stepping to the side.

"If it isn't my preppy guy, Keith. I thought you were on a vacation or something. Why back so soon?" She folded her arms leaning against the kitchen counter.

Her golden dyed hair, and big hazel irises gave her a mediocre attraction for a woman, but her plus-size body is what made most men pass. Pauline still wasn't the average girl. Even after years of knowing some of the best dealers in the city, I still haven't met a man that could stand in Pauline's shoes and flip a bird the way she can. She was like the Usain Bolt of track and field in my eyes.

"Yeah, that didn't go to well, so I had to cancel. I need some assistance with making a few more avenues, and connections to bag some new buyers. I'm asking for help from the two women I know that handle business the best."

"How much help are you looking for, Keith?" she questioned with a raised brow.

"Nine hundred thousand dollars' worth."

Clearing her throat, she asked the two girls working in the kitchen behind us to depart. After they left our presence. She changed her face to straight seriousness.

"You talking some serious loot, kiddo. You know Janet ain't been letting people move weight under our line. It's been a dolo promo for about seven months," she laid out as if denying me was an option.

"All that sounds well, but no one can make the move we can when it comes to a lot of people eating. And you know when we eat Pauline, we eat," I shot back, making her smile.

She leaned her head looking over at Smokey, who hadn't said a word since we arrived.

"What about him? Is he with your team, or just riding around to look good?"

"I thought he might be a little leverage for me today, but yes, he's my right hand. Pauline, Smokey. Smokey, Pauline."

"Wassup." He shot her the deuces, nonchalant.

I chuckled lightly to myself, knowing what was running on her brain. "Where is she?"

"In the back. Be my guest." She waved us off, and headed back for the living room, where shop was set up. I motioned for Smokey to follow me, as I trailed down the home's hallway, until I found Janet sitting on her bed, counting a bundle of bills.

"Hey, long time, no see. You got a minute?" I asked, posted in the threshold of her doorway,

"You're not the man to ask favors. What's going on?" She sat down the cash, giving me her full attention.

She was another plus-size girl, but her natural looks and aura was more than gorgeous. She was a spectacular energy, made for strictly dealing drugs. She was like the Cruella of *Dalmatians* in the game, and that was nearly throughout the entire state of Georgia.

"I'm in trouble, Janet. Nine hundred thousand dollars' worth. It's not a panic, but he's kinda shaky that I might bail. Blue ain't bailing me out." I kept all the way honest.

Her eyes looked as if she wanted to write the check herself at that moment, but I knew it wasn't just that easy. The game was cutthroat in every aspect when you played with dirty water. It was the risk we all took.

"Keith, I'll help you however I can. I can't promise it'll happen overnight, but I'm here. I'll shut down a few small spots and send the teams back on the road. Maybe like through North Carolina, Philly, DC, New York, make their way back down in Baltimore, Mississippi, New Orleans, and tag it back home. In a two-week run. I say maybe an estimate of like forty days." She looked at me like a Albert Einstein assistant for a project.

I knew I only had six weeks, and that was definitely gonna happen. I needed a way to push the extra dough to take care of Rhestay and stay on top, without losing hold of the Atlanta territory we possessed.

"Cool, what's in this for you? I'm gonna pay you well, of course, but is it anything you need handled? Any problem, or request to show my gratitude?"

My conclusion was proven to be right when she peeked her head around me to Smokey's black ass.

"I've never seen him before."

"He's my friend. Only friend. You see me, you see him." I juiced it right on up.

"That'll be cool if he kicks it for like fifteen minutes every few days with a bitch." She laughed.

I winked, turned on my crutches and moved over to my boy. I couldn't contain my smile, but I had to get him to agree.

"Say, dog, she wanna talk to you. Go kick it for a little minute, while I wait in the car."

He looked at me like I was having a panic attack, and chuckled.

"You gotta be busting my sack. That shit dead. No way."

"I'm serious, bro. We might not have a choice, if winning is anywhere on this agenda." I looked back at her, smiling as if she wasn't that bad.

I could see the anger all in his face. He still sucked it up, before huffing like a bull.

"I ain't fucking that bitch," he mumbled low, as he brushed past me.

I trucked my ass right out the door, headed for the car, and cracked up all the way. It was rare to see him take a L for us, but this was surely the ultimate payback. Making you love what you didn't want.

It was probably about twenty minutes later when I saw him storming out the front door, mad as a motherfucker. He stomped to the car like a child and hopped in the front seat with the ugly face. I started the engine, trying my best not to laugh.

"That shit ain't cool, Keith. Don't offer me off like that next time, man. Shawty ain't the one I need crawling down my back." He shivered like she was just horrible.

"Thanks, buddy ol pal. We're still gonna be rich after you hit you a big bitch." I laughed, speeding out of the parking lot.

"Yeah, yeah. Keep playing, I'll skip town on her ass. I'm only good with hustling, not lifting. I'm guessing we supposed to be really putting our faith into these two women huh?" he asked like they weren't capable to do the job.

I smirked confidently.

"I don't have a doubt that no one can do it better than them. I go off experience, not talk. They move like men in suits. I would trust them with my life.

Smokey nodded at my answer, staring off into space.

"So, when does this take effect?"

"In the next twenty-four hours." Keith smiled, turning on I-285 Expressway.

Chris Green

Chapter 22

Amber Heights Apartments

Chino

Sss… damn, Chinnoo," Monica's moans flowed through my ear like soft melodic tunes of Sade. I held on to her firm apple, handling the business from the back, while she stared back at me. Using my right hand, I slapped that ass hard, giving her a good shove.

"Mmm." She bit her bottom lip, slightly jumping.

Every thrust, she met with me perfectly, and I gripped her body savoring the moment. She released her orgasm, while I kissed and sucked, passionately caressing her breasts and nipples.

Once I felt that urge coming, I started to stand tall in her, beating it down for the count, until I released inside of her fine ass.

Rolling over on the bed, she flopped on top of me, with a few pecks of her own. I grabbed a cig from the ashtray, staring over into her ambiguous eyes.

"Are we ever gonna lock in and get serious, before you end up catching some bid or stupid shit? We been surviving, Chino. I don't know how long I can do Amber Heights," she complained.

I quickly jumped up, sliding all my clothes back on, along with placing my pistol on my hip. My phone began to vibrate just as I grabbed it from her dresser, and that's when I saw my sister's name on the screen.

"Monica, we got time to do whatever you want, ma. But remember, business is before life, it's before all. If we don't get money, we don't eat. So be easy, and let daddy be the back, while you bend open that crack." I smooched her lips, heading out the apartment.

I owned the surrounding four apartments that sat around me for security purposes, plus I was ducked off lingering in the enemy's neighborhood, taking shit over slowly, but surely.

Walking into the downstairs apartment that usually handles the weed trap, I noticed my sister, Tracey, sitting in a fold-out chair. Our three henchmen posted around the tough guy we snatched up earlier. Being that I hadn't heard from Po Boy in the past few days, the show had to go on so we could head back down to Birmingham.

"It's about time. Why the hell isn't son answering? We're just sitting here with this clown ass bozo, and he ain't spilling a bean. My mission isn't done, until T is in a casket," she stressed.

I didn't feel like hearing the irritation and complaining, so I threw a thumbs up, just to get her to shut the fuck up for about ten minutes, while I spoke to the crash dummy we held.

"Wakey, wakey, big man." I snatched the damp brown bag from his head, forcing him to heave with adrenaline.

"Calm down, calm down, my man. We can make this easy, my boy. We honestly don't wanna see you die in vain for being an ass, so show us some gratitude."

The spit that flew from his mouth onto my shirt, forced me slowly turn my head, in disappointment. Immediately, one of my goons knocked out three of his teeth with their gun. He coughed up a puddle of blood, and was cross-eyed from the assault, but gained his right mind back within the next few seconds.

"You're beefing with the wrong people, Chino. You know I've been rocking with T since we all fell in Miami. I'm loyal to who I am, nigga. Fault me for that, but I still remain solid, regardless of whether you kill me or not." He shrugged like I wasn't talking about shit.

"Cool." I pulled my strap, cocking it with the quickness, and placed it up to his skull.

He closed his eyes tightly and fidgeted, but damn sho opened them lips. "I know he got a few people that rocks out in Cabbagetown, a few on the east, but they ain't with telling me shit. You know T ain't slipping. He's noid, just like you."

I stood quietly for a second, trying to evaluate his answer, and before I could reply, Tracey moved past me with her gun in hand, placed it to Bear Cat's temple and pulled the trigger.

Boom!

The spray from the blood and brain matter caused me to turn my face, blinking to make sure the gunpowder from the bullet didn't hit me in my damn eyes.

"What the fuck, Tracey? Why not wait until we get all we can before you kill the fucking bait? We could've gotten more," I fumed, rubbing a hand across my forehead in frustration.

"Because if he did, we would've known all there is to know. He's bullshitting, so now it's time to go to phase two around this bitch. I wanna team out looking for my son every hour, and everyone dies that crosses our path, since no one seems to remember nothing. I want T's head. Then kill the rest." She jumped on her phone, walking into the kitchen.

I scrunched up my face with anger, but still knew she had last words whenever it came down to my brother's business. That was the main problem I had with how his shit was running. It was all due to work in my favor after time, but right now, her commands were stamped.

Gazing up at my three henchmen, I shook my head. "Don't come back until more are dead, and you find Po Boy. Now!"

They moved out of the front door like Pakistani soldiers, and after my mind started to kindle on the fuckery, I knew it was gonna be hard to stop me. *It's time to bring some old-fashioned death to the state of Georgia*, I thought, before placing my own call.

***

Kirkwood, east side of Atlanta

Miami T

I was sitting on the opposite side of the street, lurking behind the MARTA bus stop. A hood covered my head, and my car was parked a few feet down from me, at my people's spot. I had been waiting for this nigga to show up at this gas station, and shoot his usual dice game, and my antennas stood up when his 1979 old ass station wagon pulled up, beating some R&B.

I didn't hesitate to move across the street, once I noticed him slide up on the crap shooters. I was unnoticed, still didn't care about daylight, nor the witnesses. This was the only way to show the devious ones, family was off limits.

As I made my way on the patch of concrete, I slid up quicker than a cat, and slapped the cold steel across the side of his face.

Whack!

"Motherfuckerrrrr!" he cursed, gripping the open gash, before crashing to the ground. When he looked up into my eyes, his soul drained clean from his body in fear.

"T! Whh-w-what the fuck you doing, man?"

"I'm doing you, pussy." I kicked him in the stomach, forcing him to flop over in agony.

"You been owed a while, Guy. You pull a gun on my son while I'm in prison. Now that I've come home, your name rings about giving some people a little info about me, and Vee. Even Smokey." I put the gun to his leg, firing off a shot. *Poc*!

The loud roar forced the staring audience to finally break for cover, and this lame ass nigga stated to scream at the top of his chest when that fire touched his flesh.

"Mmmaaahhhhh. . . huummm, Fuckkk, fuck!" He shook like a leaf, hands covering him as if it was sufficient for a bulletproof vest. "Don't kill me, T. Chino didn't give me a choice, man. He running some shit, and he ain't alone man. Don't end me like this!" he begged.

"Shut the fuck up, nigga. You ain't dead...yet. But I do want you to deliver this message. Chino's ass is grass, and all the niggas that floated out the works with this idiot. Then I'm gonna come back and kill you, and this whole fucking neighborhood, the next time my family's name slides from between yo filthy ass lips. Where can I find him?" I mugged, asking him before aiming at his other leg.

Chris Green

Chapter 23

Detective Murray Brown

Two hours later

I pulled up to the scene at the gas station shooting that was aired across the radio. After taking care of a few recent calls, I was finally able to show my presence on the shitty side of town. I noticed the small-spaced groups of citizens looking on, so I knew it had to at least be half of these baseheads here, when the shooting happened. I noticed my cadet rookie officer taking notes from the shift leader as I walked under the caution tape.

"Tell me what happened here." I cut off their conversation, needing the full scoop.

"Well, sir, the victim won't speak at all. Like, I've tried the whole good cop thing, and he's like stiffer than a jar of peanuts."

I stared at the annoying punk as if he just insulted me, when I remembered he still was a baby when it came down to the law. It was the reason professionals like me came in town, to freshen shit up.

I noticed the ambulance still sitting in the lot, as detectives moved about. Moving swiftly over to the doors, I opened them up, ordering the EMS instructor out. Quickly jumping up the step, I slammed it closed and looked down at Gary "Guy" Baxter staring up at me, feeling unlucky to run into a second enemy, I would say. It was fun playing with fuckin criminals, because it was what I did best.

"So, this is like my thirtieth time telling you that death is like your fucking cousin. You can't escape me, Baxter, I told you. Not to mention, when you have warrants crawling throughout Fulton, and Dekalb County's ass crack. You couldn't even walk straight if they tried to give you a life sentence to prove the temptation for the streets wasn't shit."

"Man, come on, Murray. I been off yo scanners forever, nigger. No arrest, no nothing. You should be looking for the one who popped me, man," he pleaded in sympathy just for a break.

I straightened my suit jacket, leaning against the ambulance's wall like a boss. "You're a fucking con, idiot. There is no such thing as a break, and even if I wanted to, you wouldn't meet the fucking requirements. Now, I wanna know what happened here today, Baxter. This is pretty serious dealing with a shooting.

"You may have to be booked in for your warrants until we can sit back and find a match on the fingerprint forensics for this, man. I mean, you said you think Mr. Smokey Carter is the one that shot you, correct?" I gazed down at him with a look that dared him to deny me. He was gonna be sliding back up in Jefferson Street so fast, his cuffs were gonna turn into a pair of Rolex wristwatches.

"I'm try—"

"You're trying to catch a bid in the damn slammer if you think I'm walking away without this catch, Baxter. Answer my damn question, and if you lie, I'll be sure you never see the light of day on this earth again."

I had him by the balls and when he dropped his head, I knew I had him. "Yeah, he shot me. Smokey Carter," Guy announced before lowering his face in defeat. It was more than a loss, in my eyes. He would probably be tortured for spilling the beans, but his worthless gangsta savvy would only have to be accepted by the rejects, after the East Atlanta crew was down with him for the betrayal.

All I wanted was my man, and his name was now ringing on a high-profile case, I thought, before stepping out of the ambulance doors.

My eyes landed on my rookie officer, as if he was searching for the next step to make. I moved swiftly over to him, sparking a Marlboro cigarette out of my pack.

"I need you to call the unit and get the clerk to call the judge for a sign off. The name's Smokey Carter. I need a warrant placed on him for the aggravated assault of Gary Baxter."

"Yes, sir." He headed for the cruiser in full compliance.

This was the start of my beginning. I was gonna ensure no one took over the city I was handed down to protect.

***

Smokey

"Man, I'm good, my nigga. I don't even know why you keep asking me that question. This is a job, not hard, even this. I feel like I got a big ass sand clock on my back now, that I can't even view. I'm going hard for it regardless," I told Keith as I drove down the street towards Greenbriar Mall.

"That's cool, what you're saying from the mouth, bro. Is know you, I just want all to be smooth for us with this process. We might see even more if we can stay ahead of time. Sometimes we're just blind to our downfalls. The only way things will change, is if we let it. Remember the first chess game we played? Instead of taking our time to learn the ways of its moves, we rushed without any wisdom, and got spanked. We wanted to win so bad, any new move seemed like the best one. The choices we wanted to take so bad were in our faces the entire time. We just couldn't see them. Time makes us grow," he said at the right moment.

"And eventually we will learn to know." I smiled, finishing his sentence.

"Exactly, stop letting that petty ass shit roll in yo way. You wouldn't still be in the position if you couldn't handle it. So, whoever this Chino... Penno... guy is, he only has so much time."

"I guess you just know how to make me become the best trapper in the world, huh? Get off my line." I laughed, hanging up before pulling into the IHOP's driveway

The mall was packed, and the sun was beaming high as I made my way inside. Moving over towards the table, my eyes searched the room until I found my sweet mama, Vee, waving me over with her little hand. I could see she sported a new set of curls. She was dressed in all-black, and a pair of Chanel sandals.

"Now, you got a lot of explaining to do, boy. Why haven't you called me and let me know you feeling okay?" She hugged my neck, taking her seat.

"I've just been busy lately. I was trying to focus on getting this business open, so I can make sure you and my future wife will be cherished and loved. Somebody gotta take care of you, old lady."

Hearing *wife* made my mom's face frown up as if she didn't want to hear that step coming ahead for me in the future.

"The one thing I learned in my forty-nine years on this planet is, you can't please everybody. You always try your best to make everybody happy when some people are meant to be in their position, Smokey," she replied in a dry tone.

"Ma, it's my job to make sure everybody I say I love and care for, is straight by any means. I mean, ain't that's why we do this thing we do anyway?" I asked, sliding the cup of coffee in front of me closer.

The waitress was sitting down breakfast down for me and my mama. It was good that I could finally seek some quality time with her and needed to make it count. Living the life of a gangster left me abandoning the responsibilities of being a supporting son, in my mind.

"You sound just like yo damn father." She frowned, balling up her face at me, like I was wrong for being too overprotective.

"I mean isn't that good, Ma? I would think you'd want me to be the man he was, taking care of the family like I should be.

Dragging her nicotine, she forced a small laugh.

"I would never want you to be like him."

"What's that supposed to mean, Mama?"

"Your father took care of you and your brother, and also sacrificed certain shit to cover up his wrongs, Smokey. Money didn't ever freeze him for chumping me like a hoe when mad, neither sticking his shit in another woman. When I first met your dad, I knew I would be with him forever. That's all fine and dandy on a parent complex, but when we speak on marriage or relationships, he wouldn't even quit for the sake of losing his own family. Now, if that's what you call being a good daddy, then you might wanna recategorize your choices and thinking, before ending up with similar slip-ups."

I watched her pulling on the tobacco, and her words truly ate at me. I can feel the pain surfacing from every syllable. Something that I was never used to.

Why haven't you ever told me this before?" I asked.

"Some things are just left better unsaid, baby. The one thing I've always been guaranteed since birth is to return back to my god."

I sat for at least a good thirty minutes, sharing a meal, and conversation with the woman that blessed me with life. That moment felt better than any other thing I could've been doing at that exact time.

Feeling the phone vibrate on my hip, I checked it and quickly planted a kiss on my mama's cheek, dropping the bill on the table at the same time.

"I love you, lady. I'll see you later."

"Love you too, honey."

After leaving the eatery with my moms, I had gotten a call from a clientele on the westside, out of Bowen Homes. It was rare, that I drove all the way to the hood, to make a few hundred-dollars' play, but it was never a time where I didn't enjoy that good westside hospitality. The aura of being in the underworld and feeling proud of what you did. It was the spot where I shined, because I was supposed to be the man.

I rode smoothly to the other part of Atlanta in less than fifteen minutes. I could literally smell the ghetto rising from the concrete when you landed inside the city. I made my way through Simpson, cutting down Bankhead to reach Bowen Homes apartments. It was the dangerous of the most dangerous in this spot. I was known to keep a team whenever I pushed through, but I eventually earned my name out in the turf about being belligerent when disrespected.

I spotted my normal main connect posted by the basketball court as I pulled down inside. His green apple Chevy was parked, resting on factories, and you could tell he was probably the man out of these nigga's spot. No one owned leadership over the westside besides the ones that truly fed the westside. The real suppliers that paved a way for niggas to eat freely while they watched.

"Goddamn, Steve. What is it with the cars, my nigga? You pull somethin out different every week. It's about time to crank the car show up." I smiled, hopping out of my all-black, 4Runner truck.

"Smokey bear. You been spending mo money than the bank 'round this bitch. I was just about to call and ask you for a loan, fool." He embraced me and flexed the Submariner Rolex on his wrist. "Twenty G's, Smokey. Life is always good when you can live it how you see it."

"I guess. You know I don't go for everything I see, unless it got a dollar sign on it. I can read well."

Tossing him the nine zips of cocaine on the hood, I looked around, keeping an eye out on my surroundings.

"A-1, just as always." Steve tasted a small sample of the product and tossed it onto his front seat.

Counting out the few grand for me, I shoved it in my pocket and noticed the chain hanging around his neck. It was a pair of praying hands around a cross that read, *Gangsta For Life*. The image kind of sent chills around me at that moment, because this is one statement I've always stood against, when it came to street terminology.

"You make sure you stay safe, bro." I headed back to my car.

My next trip was to Pauline and Janet's spot to set Jo for tomorrow's road trip. A few connections needed some drop offs and we were finally getting the chance to make the extra dough, outside the eyes of Rhestay's peepers watching us.

Cranking my engine, I swerved back around to the front of the apartments, watching all the turning heads staring my car down. It was weird, a little too weird. Just as I reached the front entrance and turned to make a left, a black Mercedes Benz was bending the corner to enter. The two side windows began to roll down, releasing the barrels of a few handguns. All I could see was the face of the driver, wearing a mask, before the first slug sounded off.

Boc!

Gripping the steering wheel, I ducked, and mashed the pedal forcefully. The penetration from the other slugs began to rain like water, as I tried to make it away from the dead zone.

Boc! Bop! Boc! Boc! Boc! Boc!

Glass shattered, and the metal clinked loudly as the shots ricocheted from my whip. Lifting my head, I nearly ran into a brick wall, but slipped it by making a sharp left. Getting my car back on track, I did a hundred miles an hour down the two-way, heading for Keith's spot. I didn't know what the fuck just happened, and I wasn't about to try and stick around to find out. All I knew was that niggas wasn't playing fair with me, or my team. I was finding myself under pressure with every move we made, something that was about to stop immediately.

Chapter 24

Keith

Smokey made it to my home, explaining what had just taken place, and of course I had a few men doin the job to search for the suspects he could remember. Even though things were starting to get out of hand, I was still gonna enforce our soldiers to kill when the disrespect presented itself. It was only so much I could allow to slide, and this was one of them. I was finally sending my groups out on the road in the a.m., and in order to make sure all was gonna be perfect, we had to stay focused and think dope.

Smokey made his way back down the stairs to the living area, after grabbing a shower, and changing. I knew his energy was off balance, but now that he was shaken, we had to stamp the next steps for our operation.

"How you feeling?" I asked, checking his mode.

He shrugged. "Feel the same as always. Nothing has changed. Let's get money and delete these stupid mother-fuckers that keep aggravating my day."

"Well put." I grabbed my cell, glancing at the time. "I need everyone out on the highway in the next two hours. We move upstate, no longer than a week, we should be heading back down south, to gather any loose screws up before we stop back home. The first drop for Rhestay is in four days, and I want this to flow smoothly as possible."

"How many keys we talking 'bout getting rid of?" Smokey cut in.

"Ninety-four."

Pauline whistled, before grabbing her bag. "I can tell you this, if we don't get out of state before sunset, we're bound to have the entire patrol of whatever state and county, on our bumper with all these strong ass drugs. Timing is everything, so I'm ready to leave."

I clasped my hands, realizing everybody's stuck-up ass attitude meant they were ready to progress, so I quickly cut the small talk.

"We have nothing but each other. Let's just make this money and get back home quickly as possible."

Just as the last words escaped my mouth, the teams were breaking up, preparing to leave. I was addressing a few more things when Smokey's phone stated to ring.

"Hello?" he answered.

I could see he was quiet for a minute, but once he placed the line on speaker, I noticed he was receiving a call from the jail. It didn't take long for him to accept it and Slip Rock's voice fell through the line.

"Nephew, how you?" he asked in a smooth tone.

I knew his uncle was a legend when it came to pimping, plus I knew he was original on the block when it came to getting money in Atlanta. What I didn't know was what was about to spill from his lips.

"Smokey, the streets are talking and I need you to listen to me well. Chino is sliding through the city like a serpent, and I don't think he's trying to come for the family reunion."

"Yeah, we kind of figured that. I'm sitting right here with Keith, so you know we just wanna make sure we do what's best for everyone."

"Understood, do that by moving silent. Yo pop is back out, and that's probably the best blessing you can have right now. Cherish that and keep rising with what you doing, Smokey. Nothing else matters, nephew. Besides that, how y'all living?"

I strolled around the kitchen, nodding at the recent achievements, accepting the failures, and preparing to defeat the ones to come. I knew we gained more than we lost.

"We in the race, and I'm looking in the mirror at the guy who's in second place." I laughed.

"I'm trying to fucking tell ya," Keith chimed in with me.

We all kind of shared a laugh in unison, and that was a moment I could have paid a million dollars to catch on film. My uncle didn't only give me the right words to grind harder and kill the enemy. He gave me my mojo with enhancing at with every move I made.

"Well, make sure you stay there and never let it go. I'll be in touch but as always, stay quiet, neph," he replied, before ending the call as fast as he dialed my number.

I was surely on point with what was needed, and how to slide from that moment on. Looking at everyone else, I rubbed my hands. "Let's begin."

***

Chino

"Aye, answer the door for me." I nodded to one of my workers as we sat in the living room, closing down all our shit for a clean getaway.

Word was flowing hard that we were all at war, and the whispers of T running around here, laying down his pistol game was definitely back in effect. I had been plotting for days on how to either catch him or Smokey down bad, so I can toy with the other's mind. I needed leverage quickly.

A young hustler by the name of Shannon came spilling through the door, with a look of worry written over his face.

His shirt was all jacked up and wrinkled, plus his posture spelled uncomfortable.

"Chino, the word about that nigga people being in Cabbagetown is official. I just got word from Guy. We might need to start moving a little careful. A few thugs jumped out on me asking about you, and they meant business. Smokey is pushing some weight around obviously cause niggas is feeling the tension in the hood."

"Mmm-hmm. That's kinda funny you say Guy told you about homie's people, when my shooter clearly told me he had been caught up working with those folks. Now, either you lying like a motherfucker, or you had a little run-in with the pigs that you're trying to cover up," I said, while ripping open a cigarillo.

His vibe was shaking out his skin now, and I could see through him like a transparent blunt. I had already moved a step ahead of him to make sure he was followed, in case things didn't add up with his story.

"Naw, man, I'm just giving you the scoop how it is."

My doorman punched him in the side of the head, before he had a chance to offer any more bullshit from his mouth. Once he collapsed against the floor, he was snatched back up with the quickness.

"I think we have a problem now, Shannon, 'cause I see you don't value life, lil buddy. I gave you simple instructions, and you rebelled," I said just as Tracey walked straight into the living room, staring down at him with hatred.

The small moment of silence told me what was probably about to come next, and just as I suspected, Tracey was pulling out her .380 pistol.

"Noo!" I yelled before she sent a slug through his nose cavity.

Boc!

"He was a waste of time. I say we move out now and go rustling through these places ourselves. Time is running out, and I didn't make it this far to leave empty handed."

"We aren't empty. We have the money. We can—"

"Do nothing, but what I asked. Money doesn't mean anything to this mission. I want blood. All of it."

Feeling my brain sizzling inside my head. I smiled to keep the anger from jumping out and choking the living hell out of her. Spotting the basketball game tickets sitting on the coffee table, a nasty idea flowed through my head, causing me to form a devilish smile. Using Bear Cat's phone, I texted Smokey's number and sat back waiting patiently for a reply.

Chapter 25

Smokey

State Farm Arena / Georgia Dome

Westside, Atlanta

After leaving the Bluff on the westside and picking up a quota from a worker, Keith, Coolio and I headed down to State Farm Arena. We were going meet up with Bear Cat about the recent connection he just recently stumbled across. After getting the message from him about the new clientele, I couldn't pass up the offer with linking us all in, especially when it came with a free basketball game of the Atlanta Hawks against the Milwaukee Bucks.

"How long do you think it might be?" Keith parked, checking his wristwatch.

"I say about twenty-five to thirty minutes. We gotta get in, find the seats, and discuss all the necessary shit in between. Just keep your eyes open," I warned before jumping out with Coolio by my side.

I had my young hitta Felipe in position to make a real show soon, and I knew it would be the easiest way to flush out the skunks.

Walking into the center, the sound of the loud game could be heard from the metal detectors. Fans shouted and buzzers roared. By the time we cashed in our tickets, climbed the flight of stairs, and entered the arena the live NBA game was in effect.

"I think our section is to the left." Coolio tapped my shoulder, pointing over to the left of us.

I scanned the jam-packed stadium and followed the numbers until we found our designated row. The Hawks had possession of the ball, and it wasn't more than a minute and fifteen seconds on the clock, I felt my phone buzz. Swiftly reaching for it, I saw Bear Cat's name on the front of it and answered.

"Yo, we here, what section are you in, man?" I covered one ear to see if I could get a good reception through all the loud noise.

"I'm right here in front of you, nigga, nice to meet you, smoke dog." a strange voice spoke through the line.

My mind told me to look straight down in front of me, and once I did, my eyes landed on Chino, and Po Boy's mama Tracey, staring up at me as if I was their most prized possession. I noticed the gun coming from under his shirt rising up to me, and before I could force myself to move, the bullet from his gun let off, striking Coolio in the shoulder just as he tackled me to the floor.

The pandemonium was spiraling out of control, and basketball players, down to the fans, were scattering for safety.

"Are you okay, Smokey? Get up! We gotta get out here," he yelled, snatching me off the concrete floor.

I noticed his right arm was bleeding profusely, but he held his gun in the other hand, escorting me towards the exit. We paced, trying not to look out of the ordinary but at the moment, wasn't shit ordinary.

Getting down to the main floor, we made our way out into the parking lot. I could see Keith watching us through the windshield, as we moved back towards the car. once he realized the blood was leaking from Coolio's shirt. The car started, flushing directly towards us. Once he stopped, I snatched the door open, pushing in our shooter, and hopping in directly behind.

Just as Keith swerved the car into a U-turn, Chino and his men could be seen coming through the crowd.

"Go, go, go!" I shouted, just as the first round of shots started to release.

Keith ducked his head, flooring the pedal, and we nearly tilted on two tires coming out of the parking space.

We pushed down Northside Drive, doing the dash and all I could see in my vision was murder. Chino had to go, and I was about to make sure it happened sooner, than later.

Using my line, I dialed my hitta's number, waiting for his tone to grace the line.

"Yello, wassup with it, big man?"

"I need you to show me we've already won. Do ya thing." I gave him my honors to take off the leash.

"Until you say stop, my nigga," he replied, hanging up.

Keith was staring at me, still glancing from every outlook to see if we were being tailed. "What the fuck happened? A meeting at a basketball game turns to a shootout. What the fuck ever happened to pretzels, nachos, and that type thing. We just randomly go to the NBA games and have shootouts now?" he asked a rhetorical question like it was intentional on celebrating the Fourth of July.

"Naw, Keith, we just happened to have Elmer Fudd in the damn arena, and he just so happened to have Bear Cat's phone. I'm tired of playing with these bitches. If they want us to play games and get dirty, let's show 'em we the best at this shit." I glanced out of the window, knowing blood was about to be spilled.

***

Mama Vee

Cabbagetown

Getting a small moment to myself, I sat out on the porch for about thirty minutes. Soaking in all the good wind shifting around the air. I sipped on my warm tea, with a shot of Seagram's Gin. Days weren't the best, but at the end, I was grateful for all I was blessed with. My husband and son was back at home. Even though, it wasn't on the best of terms, it was just enough to see them back under the same room.

Tracy stepping outside on her porch, forced me to turn my head.

"Hey, Vee, how you holding, hun?" She sat directly beside me in a picnic chair.

"Whew, child, I'm trying the best I can, girl. You know how they say, you ain't been through nothing, if you ain't struggled with something."

"If that ain't the truth, we always go through our tough situations when our blessings are close by, queen. You just gotta make them motherfuckas kiss ya ass, and smile where they can keep moving past you."

I had to ponder on what she what saying. Life was nothing without challenges. I had been through so much on the past few years, I didn't know how the world would bend for me in my time of need. I was more than a strong black woman. I was a confident one, but the street life in Atlanta was one I didn't need destroying my family legacy to live on.

"I feel like that's the truth half the time, Tracy. After experiencing so much, I've molded myself to accept life, but fight for what was right. I can't keep sitting back, waiting the same song, play to the same damn tune. Truly, I just want better for the kids." I thought about my babies, resting peacefully in the house.

Our conversation was split in half from the black Mercedes Benz pulling up slowly in the lot. Tracy's hand moved towards that big ass .357 resting beside her. We were stiff, with no motion, when the all the doors popped open simultaneously. I immediately got behind her, and she didn't hesitate to step forward with her gun, finger semi-wrapped around the trigger in case stupidity arose.

When I watched Chino step out of the car with two armed men, and that maggot ass girl who I despised, I nearly flipped in the air. "They're here for me, please don't kick me out!" I pleaded, thinking this white lady was about to turn racist, and throw us to the wolves.

"Go in the house," she mumbled to me, but my feet just couldn't move.

Small groups of civilians stood outside in silence, and a few rednecks protruded outside their doorways, watching intently.

"If it ain't white, it ain't right," a male voice spoke from a distance.

I watched Chino hold up his hands in surrender, with a wicked smile. "Please, we come in peace. We're only looking for the little thing hiding behind you, and we'll be on our way. We don't need any violence, or negativity to break out in the air," he tried to reason.

"I'll tell you people like this here. This is my neighborhood, and nothing booms through this spot unless it goes through me. Now, this little thing you say behind me, is family, so if you have trouble with her, you have trouble with me."

I knew I hadn't seen shit, until I watched a buff ass white man, with a mohawk come from behind her home, with an M-16 assault rifle around his neck and arms.

"Tracy, do we have a problem around here? We got a few lost ones, don't we?" He spat loudly on the ground, cracking his neck from side to side.

Tattoos covered most of his belly and neck, and judging from the veins protruding from his neck and chest, he was more than likely higher than a kite.

"Naw, bubba, we just gotta couple of bozos that don't know any better when it comes down to family. We go all in for ours, but I think they were just leaving, if I'm not mistaken."

Now a few more doors in the neighborhood slid open. Guns were being pulled left to right, and what I thought was a set up to kill me, turned into more of a standoff with Chino and Tracey barely leaving with their lives intact, if it wasn't for the mercy of God.

Chino nodded, as he stared around at all the neighbors, glaring down at them with malice, ready to be written in front of murder.

"I see what you mean, snow. We don't have a problem letting what's said be done for now, but you can't possibly think you're gonna be around forever?" he asked, while pulling his conniving sister with him.

Tracy never responded with anything but a smirk, and nod from her revolver. At that moment, I was truly grateful to have her beside me, because it was ticking near my time to be tried. I had suffered, and lost so much, that all I wanted was for the chaos to end.

"You're gonna be okay, hun. T is a friend, and we help friends over this way. Your blood is like my blood," she said sincerely, guiding me into the apartment for safety.

"I'll call a few friends to keep an eye out front. Just ease yourself." She bounced up the stairs to check on the children.

I wasted no time using my phone to dial Smokey's number. It didn't take him long to answer.

"Wassup, Mama?"

"I need you to find us somewhere to go. These people know where we are, Smokey. They pulled up over here to her home," I stressed.

"What! And what happened?" he shouted recklessly.

"Well, Tracy ran them off, with a few help from her neighborhood hoodlums. They really didn't have a chance, but I'm scared."

"Hey, Mama, I need you to stay focused for me. Right now, if I take the chances on moving you, we might not be lucky enough to make it where we need to. If Tracy is able to look out for you, with a slight form of protection, you might need to stay put. It's too much going on for me to risk you being safe."

I had to listen to my son's plea, and understand where he was coming from, but I still didn't want to accept the fact that we were stuck in the tar of a beef, and a cheating ass father of his. A pointless act that was placing the name of our family at jeopardy. I didn't want to see it end that horrible way.

"Okay, Smokey. I'll listen." My mind said to go against that shit immediately.

"Thank you, I'll call my dad to make sure he stays on point. You're gonna be fine. I can promise you."

"Bye," I responded before pressing the end button.

I knew for a fact I had more than one problem, and that was my son and crazy ass husband, causing more drama than the city could actually see. I just prayed I didn't lose them in the process.

Chris Green

Chapter 26

Detective Murray Brown

Zone 6 Precinct

It was around 8:30 this morning when I received the call from my superior to get down to the station immediately. According to a few rookies, a bomb threat had been called in, forcing all the officers on duty, to be placed on sit with no movements, until reinforcements came with backup.

Hopping out of the car, I made my way through the caution tape, and approached the captain.

"Sir, what's going on?"

"Brown, we have a bomb threat in progress. I've called all the reinforcements for back-up, and the FBI and ATF is ready to snatch this case right from under our noses. We need to find the next best solution to keep this thing under our control, before we lose it all," he answered, rubbing a hand across his chin.

Numerous of deputies stood about preparing to take action in case the event of having to save a life presented itself

"Suit me up, Captain. I have enough credentials to go in, and deactivate it, if it is a live explosive. I'll take a double man for cover, and handle this on my own. No one can pull this off but me," I spoke truthfully.

He took a second to reply, and just when I thought he would shut me out, he proved me different.

"Hey, Clark, suit up Brown for *Operation Set Up*. I want the best two going in with him to ensure he's okay. Put the gear on him."

"But, sir, we're not clear on what we're dealing with here. If he goes in blindly, not knowing what's ahead. It could potentially put us all at risk."

"I said, suit him up, Clark!" he yelled a little louder this time, to enforce his authority.

I slightly smiled, knowing I was a golden child when it came to having my way with the department. It was my duty to protect and serve, and I was gonna handle the job by any means.

After dressing up in the thick, bomb squad gear, I placed my first foot on the concrete, moving straight towards the black rectangular suitcase, resting on the precinct steps.

I could feel the tension rising, as me, and the other two deputies moved slowly towards the target. A nine-millimeter pistol in my left hand. It had been years since I was overseas, war active in the field, deactivate bombs for my next badge. It was a reality I was living all over again and that's what made every moment so surreal.

By the time I reached the large bag, I channeled in, every detail I seen, and pulled my utensils, to undo the zipper. I slowly slid it back until it was fully open and breathed in calmly. When I flipped the top fold, the first thing my sight caught was the severed, and battered head of a man. I could tell the large stench coming from inside, meant that the rest of him was surely underneath. I nearly puked, and the officers behind me, didn't even think of coming any closer after realizing what I recently discovered.

Hitting the button on my radio, I called for the captain.

"Sir, we got a problem."

"What is it, Brown? Can you stop it?"

"It's not a bomb, sir. It's a body. A dismembered one if I might say," my words fell out dryly.

"Shittt! I gotta call in the feds." He ended the radio, leaving me to myself.

Taking off my helmet cover, I inhaled for some fresh air, as I stared into the dead eyes of the familiar face. Something was telling me this was a message, and not a regular homicide. The feeling that a war was about to take off in the city was bubbling, and I could feel that if was about to blow soon. I just didn't know with who.

***

Smokey

Out of all the days, this was the most laid back. My birthday was finally here, and this was damn sho about to be a party, where I can soak up some fun and truly remember I do have a life. I had paid for a mobile escort tonight for me and my team to hit the club and shine at our best. I was dressed in a pair of J.M. Weston's, a Louis Vuitton two-piece, pinstriped suit, and a few pieces of nice rose gold to top it off. I had invited a few people to a private get-together at The Jaguar over in Fourth Ward. A nice spot popular for known hood figures coming to kick it. I was twenty years old, and I didn't need nothing ruining today for some peace.

"Wassup, my guy? Can we please head the hell up out of here? I'm not trying to be fighting traffic with all these people tonight," Keith said, while I double checked my appearance in the mirror.

"Yeah, we out this bitch," I answered, checking to make sure gear was on point. "I didn't want no slipping on my day, ya feel me."

"That's all good, my soul brudda, but let's try making this runway model look on to the car, so we can be out of here."

I laughed like hell, making my way up out of the condo, I purchased a few months back. It wasn't too many places I wanted to lay my head, so only a few knew of the location. I only used it for certain purposes, but after the recent things that had started to transpire, I moved my mama, and them over, to get a slight distance from our usual grounds of turf. It had been a few days since we slid our crews on the roads to deliver every order possible. Shit was slowly forming back together. I had gotten the news from Felipe, that my job for him went well, and that was probably the only thing keeping me at bay.

It didn't take long for us to reach the other side of town, over in Fourth Ward. The club was live, the air was breezing smoothly, and everything lined up in the parking lot, looked like it was birthed from a dollar. You could literally smell the paper lingering in the air.

As me and my crew stepped out, we caught the center of all attention. I just didn't know I had the wrong eyes on me at that moment. I posed for a few pictures and brushed straight through the VIP line as we headed inside.

The Jaguar was filled with all kinds of life. Lights illuminated across the walls, and the vibrant music bounced off the walls louder than a baseball field. Yo Gotti, and Rylo Rodriguez hit single for me was sliding through the tweeters, and I had to say the vibe was tight, and on point.

"Y'all niggas give a big shout out to my man, Smokey Carter, for his twentieth birthday. He the east side Biggie Smallz around the block, and if you talking about money, that's a problem he can come stop. Enjoy your day, big dawg. Live it up," the DJ screamed through the booth speakers.

I trailed over to the private section where my family, friends and few associates sat, and joined my gathering. I was instantly surrounded by love and gifts, and before I knew it, I was drinking, passing champagne bottles, and bobbing my head to the street music bumping.

"So, out of all the nights you been able to catch ya breath and rest, can you say this is one of the best?" Keith asked me, as we shared a drink, and toast to the accomplishments.

I knew for a fact it was the most money I had ever spent or made in my life. It was the hardest I've ever hustled to perfection. I was literally the man in my hood, my city. I was the plug.

"I feel like it's exactly where I'm supposed to be, at the exact moment. I'm grateful." I held up the champagne flute.

"You deserve it. We just gotta make sure it last forever," Keith added.

My ears listened closely to his words, and I knew I had a true friend standing beside me. We truly came from juvenile catching minor charges, to touching the streets, standing in the kitchen. It was the life of a lives. The fast one.

"Guess what, Keith" It never lasts that long. We just make sure when we do it. We make it long enough to last us forever when it ends. It's the game, baby boy, and we always know the game has a timer. We locked in like two flat tires on the same street."

He shared a laugh with me, as we looked on at the crowd grinded and moved to the music. I enjoyed the best of foods. Sliced one of the most delicious cakes I've ever tasted in my life, and out of nowhere my entire evening was struck by beauty would change my life forever. It was like an angel appearing right in front of me, when I turned around to head for the bathroom.

Her hair was black, curled at the edges, hanging gently to the small of her back. Her lovely eyes were wide, dark brown, viewing all the life with gentleness in the room. She was curvy in all the right places, dressed in a Gucci silk dress trimmed in gold lining. Of course, her feet were looking more beautiful than ever, stepping in a pair of white six-inch pumps. She was the epitome of a gorgeous black goddess, and definitely struck me with a heart of love from first sight.

"Hey." I forced my lips to speak and delete the slight paranoia that was dangling at the back of my conscious mind.

"Hi," she replied back, immediately with a bright, thirty-two-tooth smile. Her dimples were deep as the Grand Canyon, and I couldn't tell where she had come from, but my mind kept telling me to proceed, by grabbing her hand.

Just as she tried to walk away, during our moment of silence. I reached out for her fingers.

"I don't mean to be pushy, beautiful, but what type of man would I be if I allow you to just leave me standing here alone like that?"

She gazed at me, up and down, scanning my persona like a love radar expert. I had never witnessed a chick so natural, and classy.

"I'm not sure, sir, maybe a crazy one, but probably a smart one if you've ever said that line to anybody else," she shot back with a sexy smirk.

I was head over heels for this sweet girl already and she hadn't even been in my presence for a full day. She was standing in front of me, looking edible, when I took her hand and twirled her in a full spin.

"A woman like you shouldn't even be in here like this. I know your husband would probably be furious if he knew how much I was stunned by you. I could just snatch you up and take you to paradise right now."

"Mmm, that's a trip I haven't experienced, but they say God is the planner of all that, king. Do you have a name?" she asked with a raised brow, as if I were a little child.

Her innocent, beauty had me flabbergasted. A magnificent woman was rare, but for some reason I knew that I had just found mines.

"Uhh, my name is Smokey, love. Smokey Carter. What about yourself?"

"My name is Simone, straight from this wonderful soil we call Atlanta, GA."

"Do you have a moment to sit and give me a little sec to find out more about you? I mean, I would like to have more time with you to speak. . . if like, you weren't busy?"

She studied me for a second, before opening her lips to reply. "I'm single, yes. I'm only nineteen, working for all I need in this world. I'm not used to a man telling the truth about anything but his own needs, and cares, so words don't amaze me, but you are very handsome and approached me well. Shall I explain more?" she said with savvy laced inside her words.

I smirked at her arrogance and held out my arm for her to follow.

"If you don't mind, I'm having a little after party at my spot for my birthday. I would like it if you come meet a few family members, and friends of mine. I'm sure we should have a few associates in common, or at least a hobby or two. What do you say? Can I get you to join a lonely birthday boy for his after party?"

"Maybe, depending on if you can behave yourself, young man. I see a fire inside of you I'm not too sure about. Tell me more." She accepted my arm and began to walk with me.

I was smiling ear to ear, as I quickly ended my night and prepared to alert my guest that we were about to disperse from The Jaguar and go back to my condo.

"I can tell you all you wanna know. Right this way, queen," I said politely, heading through the crowd.

After me and Keith gathered up together, we bundled up in the cars, and left out of the lot, feeling better than ever. I was posted with my arm around Simone and enjoying our light conversation, when the sight of an approaching car caught my vision. As it slowed down coming near us, the sight of a gun barrel came hanging gently out the window. I didn't have time to shout, all I could do was try and push Simone to the ground, covering her before the slugs started to rain hard.

Bloom! *Bloom*! *Bloom*! *Bloom*! *Bloom*!

I felt a bullet strike my back hard, and the next one tagged my right shoulder. Simone's screams were loud as the shells tore against the car. I silently prayed we made it through this, as I glanced at the front seat, where Keith ducked for his life. I felt my heart thump heavily. I inhaled a deep breath and after a few seconds, the gunshots stopped, the smoke was clear, but no one was talking.

To Be Continued. . .

The Plug of Lil Mexico 2: Even the Odds
Coming Soon

Lock Down Publications and Ca$h Presents assisted publishing packages.

BASIC PACKAGE $499
Editing
Cover Design
Formatting

UPGRADED PACKAGE $800
Typing
Editing
Cover Design
Formatting

ADVANCE PACKAGE $1,200
Typing
Editing
Cover Design
Formatting
Copyright registration
Proofreading
Upload book to Amazon

LDP SUPREME PACKAGE $1,500
Typing
Editing
Cover Design
Formatting
Copyright registration
Proofreading
Set up Amazon account

Chris Green

Upload book to Amazon
Advertise on LDP Amazon and Facebook page

***Other services available upon request. Additional charges may apply
Lock Down Publications
P.O. Box 944
Stockbridge, GA 30281-9998
Phone # 470 303-9761

Submission Guideline

Submit the first three chapters of your completed manuscript to ldpsubmissions@gmail.com, subject line: Your book's title. The manuscript must be in a .doc file and sent as an attachment. Document should be in Times New Roman, double spaced and in size 12 font. Also, provide your synopsis and full contact information. If sending multiple submissions, they must each be in a separate email.

Have a story but no way to send it electronically? You can still submit to LDP/Ca$h Presents. Send in the first three chapters, written or typed, of your completed manuscript to:

LDP: Submissions Dept
Po Box 944
Stockbridge, Ga 30281

DO NOT send original manuscript. Must be a duplicate.

Provide your synopsis and a cover letter containing your full contact information.

Thanks for considering LDP and Ca$h Presents.

<u>NEW RELEASES</u>

GRIMEY WAYS by RAY VINCI
A GANGSTA SAVED XMAS by MONET DRAGUN
XMAS WITH AN ATL SHOOTER by CA$H & DESTINY
SKAI
CUM FOR ME by SUGAR E. WALLZ
THE BRICK MAN 3 by KING RIO
THE PLUG OF LIL MEXICO by CHRIS GREEN

Coming Soon from Lock Down Publications/Ca$h Presents

BLOOD OF A BOSS **VI**

SHADOWS OF THE GAME II

TRAP BASTARD II

By **Askari**

LOYAL TO THE GAME **IV**

By **T.J. & Jelissa**

IF TRUE SAVAGE **VIII**

MIDNIGHT CARTEL IV

DOPE BOY MAGIC IV

CITY OF KINGZ III

NIGHTMARE ON SILENT AVE II

THE PLUG OF LIL MEXICO II

By **Chris Green**

BLAST FOR ME **III**

A SAVAGE DOPEBOY III

CUTTHROAT MAFIA III

DUFFLE BAG CARTEL VII

HEARTLESS GOON VI

By **Ghost**

A HUSTLER'S DECEIT III

KILL ZONE II

BAE BELONGS TO ME III

By **Aryanna**

KING OF THE TRAP III

By **T.J. Edwards**

GORILLAZ IN THE BAY V

3X KRAZY III

STRAIGHT BEAST MODE II

De'Kari

KINGPIN KILLAZ IV

STREET KINGS III

PAID IN BLOOD III

CARTEL KILLAZ IV

DOPE GODS III

Hood Rich

SINS OF A HUSTLA II

ASAD

RICH $AVAGE II

MONEY IN THE GRAVE II

By Martell Troublesome Bolden

YAYO V

Bred In The Game 2

S. Allen

CREAM III

By Yolanda Moore

SON OF A DOPE FIEND III

HEAVEN GOT A GHETTO II

By Renta

LOYALTY AIN'T PROMISED III

By Keith Williams

I'M NOTHING WITHOUT HIS LOVE II

SINS OF A THUG II

TO THE THUG I LOVED BEFORE II

The Plug of Lil Mexico

By Monet Dragun
QUIET MONEY IV
EXTENDED CLIP III
THUG LIFE IV
By **Trai'Quan**
THE STREETS MADE ME IV
By **Larry D. Wright**
IF YOU CROSS ME ONCE II
By **Anthony Fields**
THE STREETS WILL NEVER CLOSE II
By K'ajji
HARD AND RUTHLESS III
THE BILLIONAIRE BENTLEYS II
Von Diesel
KILLA KOUNTY II
By Khufu
MONEY GAME III
By Smoove Dolla
JACK BOYZ VERSUS DOPE BOYZ
By Romell Tukes
MURDA WAS THE CASE II
Elijah R. Freeman
THE STREETS NEVER LET GO II
By Robert Baptiste
AN UNFORESEEN LOVE III
By **Meesha**
KING OF THE TRENCHES II

Chris Green

by **GHOST & TRANAY ADAMS**

MONEY MAFIA II

LOYAL TO THE SOIL II

By **Jibril Williams**

QUEEN OF THE ZOO II

By **Black Migo**

THE BRICK MAN IV

By King Rio

VICIOUS LOYALTY II

By Kingpen

A GANGSTA'S PAIN II

By J-Blunt

CONFESSIONS OF A JACKBOY III

By Nicholas Lock

GRIMEY WAYS II

By Ray Vinci

<u>Available Now</u>

RESTRAINING ORDER **I & II**

By **CA\$H & Coffee**

LOVE KNOWS NO BOUNDARIES **I II & III**

By **Coffee**

RAISED AS A GOON I, II, III & IV

The Plug of Lil Mexico

BRED BY THE SLUMS I, II, III

BLAST FOR ME I & II

ROTTEN TO THE CORE I II III

A BRONX TALE I, II, III

DUFFLE BAG CARTEL I II III IV V VI

HEARTLESS GOON I II III IV V

A SAVAGE DOPEBOY I II

DRUG LORDS I II III

CUTTHROAT MAFIA I II

KING OF THE TRENCHES

By **Ghost**

LAY IT DOWN **I & II**

LAST OF A DYING BREED I II

BLOOD STAINS OF A SHOTTA I & II III

By **Jamaica**

LOYAL TO THE GAME I II III

LIFE OF SIN I, II III

By **TJ & Jelissa**

BLOODY COMMAS I & II

SKI MASK CARTEL I II & III

KING OF NEW YORK I II,III IV V

RISE TO POWER I II III

COKE KINGS I II III IV V

BORN HEARTLESS I II III IV

KING OF THE TRAP I II

By **T.J. Edwards**

IF LOVING HIM IS WRONG...I & II

Chris Green

LOVE ME EVEN WHEN IT HURTS I II III

By **Jelissa**

WHEN THE STREETS CLAP BACK I & II III

THE HEART OF A SAVAGE I II III

MONEY MAFIA

LOYAL TO THE SOIL

By **Jibril Williams**

A DISTINGUISHED THUG STOLE MY HEART I II & III

LOVE SHOULDN'T HURT I II III IV

RENEGADE BOYS I II III IV

PAID IN KARMA I II III

SAVAGE STORMS I II

AN UNFORESEEN LOVE I II

By **Meesha**

A GANGSTER'S CODE I &, II III

A GANGSTER'S SYN I II III

THE SAVAGE LIFE I II III

CHAINED TO THE STREETS I II III

BLOOD ON THE MONEY I II III

A GANGSTA'S PAIN

By **J-Blunt**

PUSH IT TO THE LIMIT

By **Bre' Hayes**

BLOOD OF A BOSS **I, II, III, IV, V**

SHADOWS OF THE GAME

TRAP BASTARD

By **Askari**

The Plug of Lil Mexico

THE STREETS BLEED MURDER **I, II & III**

THE HEART OF A GANGSTA I II& III

By **Jerry Jackson**

CUM FOR ME I II III IV V VI VII VIII

An **LDP Erotica Collaboration**

BRIDE OF A HUSTLA **I II & II**

THE FETTI GIRLS **I, II& III**

CORRUPTED BY A GANGSTA I, II III, IV

BLINDED BY HIS LOVE

THE PRICE YOU PAY FOR LOVE I, II ,III

DOPE GIRL MAGIC I II III

By **Destiny Skai**

WHEN A GOOD GIRL GOES BAD

By **Adrienne**

THE COST OF LOYALTY I II III

By Kweli

A GANGSTER'S REVENGE **I II III & IV**

THE BOSS MAN'S DAUGHTERS I II III IV V

A SAVAGE LOVE **I & II**

BAE BELONGS TO ME I II

A HUSTLER'S DECEIT I, II, III

WHAT BAD BITCHES DO I, II, III

SOUL OF A MONSTER I II III

KILL ZONE

A DOPE BOY'S QUEEN I II III

By **Aryanna**

A KINGPIN'S AMBITON

Chris Green

A KINGPIN'S AMBITION **II**
I MURDER FOR THE DOUGH
By **Ambitious**
TRUE SAVAGE I II III IV V VI VII
DOPE BOY MAGIC I, II, III
MIDNIGHT CARTEL I II III
CITY OF KINGZ I II
NIGHTMARE ON SILENT AVE
THE PLUG OF LIL MEXICO II

By **Chris Green**
A DOPEBOY'S PRAYER
By **Eddie "Wolf" Lee**
THE KING CARTEL **I, II & III**
By **Frank Gresham**
THESE NIGGAS AIN'T LOYAL **I, II & III**
By **Nikki Tee**
GANGSTA SHYT **I II &III**
By **CATO**
THE ULTIMATE BETRAYAL
By **Phoenix**
BOSS'N UP **I , II & III**
By **Royal Nicole**
I LOVE YOU TO DEATH
By **Destiny J**
I RIDE FOR MY HITTA
I STILL RIDE FOR MY HITTA

The Plug of Lil Mexico

By **Misty Holt**

LOVE & CHASIN' PAPER

By **Qay Crockett**

TO DIE IN VAIN

SINS OF A HUSTLA

By **ASAD**

BROOKLYN HUSTLAZ

By **Boogsy Morina**

BROOKLYN ON LOCK I & II

By **Sonovia**

GANGSTA CITY

By **Teddy Duke**

A DRUG KING AND HIS DIAMOND I & II III

A DOPEMAN'S RICHES

HER MAN, MINE'S TOO I, II

CASH MONEY HO'S

THE WIFEY I USED TO BE I II

By **Nicole Goosby**

TRAPHOUSE KING **I II & III**

KINGPIN KILLAZ I II III

STREET KINGS I II

PAID IN BLOOD **I II**

CARTEL KILLAZ I II III

DOPE GODS I II

By **Hood Rich**

LIPSTICK KILLAH **I, II, III**

CRIME OF PASSION I II & III

Chris Green

FRIEND OR FOE I II III

By **Mimi**

STEADY MOBBN' **I, II, III**

THE STREETS STAINED MY SOUL I II

By **Marcellus Allen**

WHO SHOT YA **I, II, III**

SON OF A DOPE FIEND I II

HEAVEN GOT A GHETTO

Renta

GORILLAZ IN THE BAY **I II III IV**

TEARS OF A GANGSTA I II

3X KRAZY I II

STRAIGHT BEAST MODE

DE'KARI

TRIGGADALE I II III

MURDAROBER WAS THE CASE

Elijah R. Freeman

GOD BLESS THE TRAPPERS I, II, III

THESE SCANDALOUS STREETS I, II, III

FEAR MY GANGSTA I, II, III IV, V

THESE STREETS DON'T LOVE NOBODY I, II

BURY ME A G I, II, III, IV, V

A GANGSTA'S EMPIRE I, II, III, IV

THE DOPEMAN'S BODYGAURD I II

THE REALEST KILLAZ I II III

THE LAST OF THE OGS I II III

Tranay Adams

THE STREETS ARE CALLING

Duquie Wilson

MARRIED TO A BOSS I II III

By Destiny Skai & Chris Green

KINGZ OF THE GAME I II III IV V VI

Playa Ray

SLAUGHTER GANG I II III

RUTHLESS HEART I II III

By Willie Slaughter

FUK SHYT

By Blakk Diamond

DON'T F#CK WITH MY HEART I II

By Linnea

ADDICTED TO THE DRAMA I II III

IN THE ARM OF HIS BOSS II

By Jamila

YAYO I II III IV

A SHOOTER'S AMBITION I II

BRED IN THE GAME

By S. Allen

TRAP GOD I II III

RICH $AVAGE

MONEY IN THE GRAVE I II

By Martell Troublesome Bolden

FOREVER GANGSTA

GLOCKS ON SATIN SHEETS I II

By Adrian Dulan

Chris Green

TOE TAGZ I II III

LEVELS TO THIS SHYT I II

By Ah'Million

KINGPIN DREAMS I II III

By Paper Boi Rari

CONFESSIONS OF A GANGSTA I II III IV

CONFESSIONS OF A JACKBOY I II

By Nicholas Lock

I'M NOTHING WITHOUT HIS LOVE

SINS OF A THUG

TO THE THUG I LOVED BEFORE

A GANGSTA SAVED XMAS

By Monet Dragun

CAUGHT UP IN THE LIFE I II III

THE STREETS NEVER LET GO

By Robert Baptiste

NEW TO THE GAME I II III

MONEY, MURDER & MEMORIES I II III

By **Malik D. Rice**

LIFE OF A SAVAGE I II III

A GANGSTA'S QUR'AN I II III

MURDA SEASON I II III

GANGLAND CARTEL I II III

CHI'RAQ GANGSTAS I II III

KILLERS ON ELM STREET I II III

JACK BOYZ N DA BRONX I II III

A DOPEBOY'S DREAM I II III

The Plug of Lil Mexico

By **Romell Tukes**

LOYALTY AIN'T PROMISED I II

By Keith Williams

QUIET MONEY I II III

THUG LIFE I II III

EXTENDED CLIP I II

By **Trai'Quan**

THE STREETS MADE ME I II III

By **Larry D. Wright**

THE ULTIMATE SACRIFICE I, II, III, IV, V, VI

KHADIFI

IF YOU CROSS ME ONCE

ANGEL I II

IN THE BLINK OF AN EYE

By **Anthony Fields**

THE LIFE OF A HOOD STAR

By Ca$h & Rashia Wilson

THE STREETS WILL NEVER CLOSE

By K'ajji

CREAM I II

By Yolanda Moore

NIGHTMARES OF A HUSTLA I II III

By King Dream

CONCRETE KILLA I II

VICIOUS LOYALTY

By Kingpen

HARD AND RUTHLESS I II

Chris Green

MOB TOWN 251
THE BILLIONAIRE BENTLEYS
By Von Diesel
GHOST MOB
Stilloan Robinson
MOB TIES I II III IV
By SayNoMore
BODYMORE MURDERLAND I II III
By Delmont Player
FOR THE LOVE OF A BOSS
By C. D. Blue
MOBBED UP I II III IV
THE BRICK MAN I II III
By King Rio
KILLA KOUNTY
By Khufu
MONEY GAME I II
By Smoove Dolla
A GANGSTA'S KARMA I II
By FLAME
KING OF THE TRENCHES II
by **GHOST & TRANAY ADAMS**
QUEEN OF THE ZOO
By **Black Migo**
GRIMEY WAYS
By Ray Vinci
XMAS WITH AN ATL SHOOTER

The Plug of Lil Mexico

By Ca$h & Destiny Skai

<u>BOOKS BY LDP'S CEO, CA$H</u>

TRUST IN NO MAN

TRUST IN NO MAN 2

TRUST IN NO MAN 3

BONDED BY BLOOD

SHORTY GOT A THUG

THUGS CRY

THUGS CRY 2

THUGS CRY 3

TRUST NO BITCH

TRUST NO BITCH 2

TRUST NO BITCH 3

TIL MY CASKET DROPS

RESTRAINING ORDER

RESTRAINING ORDER 2

IN LOVE WITH A CONVICT

LIFE OF A HOOD STAR

XMAS WITH AN ATL SHOOTER

The Plug of Lil Mexico

CPSIA information can be obtained
at www.ICGtesting.com
Printed in the USA
LVHW081556260122
709351LV00032B/252

9 781955 270793